BLACK AND WHITE

"Don't go, Esther. Stay a minute and talk to me." His blue eyes mocked her, as he added, "Don't tell me you're afraid of me!"

Suddenly she was trembling with rage. "No, I'm not afraid of you! I'm sorry for you! You white men think all you have to do is take, take, take."

Then she was running down the hall. But he caught her and was tearing at her uniform, humbling her.

They fought silently, her nails ripping the skin from his cheeks, his chest. Desperately she was reaching for something to kill him with.

But there was nothing. Only his hard body with its unbelievable strength and intent . . .

ESTHER

A Novel by
MARY ELIZABETH VROMAN

ESTHER

A Bantam Book / published July 1963

Library of Congress Catalog Card Number: 63-14175
All rights reserved.
© Copyright, 1963, by Mary Elizabeth Vroman Gibson.
Published simultaneously in the United States and Canada.

Esther

Chapter One

IT SEEMED later to Esther Kennedy that all her life began on that Friday in June. It was as if she had slept and dreamed, happily enough, through her childhood; then on this day when she was exactly thirteen and a half she awoke to discover herself alive, aware.

The clock on the mantel said that it was exactly five when she awoke—instantly and widely awake, and wondering why, since she was usually still drowsy when Grandear called her at seven. Perhaps it was because that day she was to graduate from the eighth grade and wear the new white dress. A new, store-bought dress was something to be elated about, since Grandear frugally cut down everything she could of Lucy's to fit her.

She lay still for a while, examining the feeling. It was more than she ought to feel about graduating and a new dress. Something inside her was shining and waiting, or at least waiting to shine, the way a lightning bug might wait for the night when it could shine by itself, not needing the daylight. Or maybe flowers felt like that when they were growing, waiting to open and feeling the growing stirring and moving, bursting out from inside. "I'm alive!" she whispered with an acute sense of discovery, and giggled because it was a silly thing to be saying.

Lucy stirred in the bed that was twin to hers, and then turned on her side toward Esther. Her mouth was open; her small, dark face vacant in sleep—withdrawn. One of her thick black braids had loosened and half covered her face. Lucy was fifteen, but when she slept she looked much younger. Even awake, there was something in Lucy that made Esther think of her as younger rather than older. Perhaps because Lucy suffered from attacks of asthma and took a lot of caring for. Poor Lucy! Esther doubted that she'd ever had the singing, shining, waiting feeling. It would frighten her. Lucy was frightened of practically everything—most of all, feelings.

Esther knew now why she had been waiting. She used a

tentative tissue to make sure. Then she rose swiftly and noise-lessly and went to her grandmother's room.

Lydia Jones awoke instantly, as was her way. Even in the middle of the night, she'd be up the moment the knock came. "I hears you, Frank Taylor! Don't need to knock like that and wake up my girls. That baby o' yourn ain't coming 'fore I get there. After seven young'uns you ought not to be so anxious nohow!"

That had been the night before. She said now, "What's the matter, Esther? You sick, to be up so early?"

If Esther waited a minute Grandear would tell her. Her grandmother swung herself out of the high, old-fashioned bed, her lean, wiry body barely visible through the cotton nightgown. Her thinning, kinky hair was braided into two grey plaits that hung down to her shoulders. Against the grey of the hair and the white of the gown her face seemed blacker, sharp and drawn, old, except for the brown eyes, which were bright as a girl's. She peered at Esther, standing at the foot of the bed, and gave a small, gratified chuckle. "No, you ain't sick. You done started your womanhood. Right?"

Esther nodded.

"Well, it sure is time! Ain't no use looking like the cat what swallowed the bird about it. You's mighty late for a colored girl, and that's the truth!"

As she spoke she pulled out the top drawer of the bu-reau. "Here's all you going to need. I done told you how to use it. Here, I'll help you. Mind you bathes good every day now, when your time is on you. Put some baking soda in your wash water. Never did hold with the lies some folks tell about bathing during your days. You wash good, you hear?"

"Yes'm." Esther was embarrassed, and that too was a new feeling. She looked steadily at the floor while her grand-mother adjusted the napkin.

"My mind is much relieved," Grandear continued calmly. "Lucy, she started at ten. I was 'bout to take you to the doctor. But I just hate them white doctors messing with our folks. Treats you like pigs! What this poor, half-ass, southern town needs is a good colored doctor. 'Course, if we had one, I guess folks wouldn't be needing an old midwife like me so much." A mischievous smile flickered over her face, and for the moment she looked less than her seventy-six years.

It was over. Esther let the gown fall again into place.

Grandear said sharply, "How come you didn't mess your gown?"

"Because I was awake when it started."

Her grandmother scrutinized her face. Esther met her eyes now, the new aliveness and awareness leaping out of her in love for the old woman.

Lydia Jones sat abruptly on the bed, still looking at her. She said, strangely, "When Lucy started I didn't say much to her. She don't need no whole lot of instructions. She will do like I tells her until she gets married. Then she will do like her husband tells her. But with you now, Esther, it's different. I've watched you all these years, growing faster'n a rabbit and all full of life. You ain't exactly pretty; but you're the spit of your father with them wild, big eyes, so full of living it don't matter what you look like."

"Do I really look like him, Grandear?"

"Don't interrupt me. Now you's 'bout to be a woman, I'm feared for you. Your sister don't love life like you do, so she'll be careful, cautious-like. And life cain't hurt them that's cautious much. But you thinks life is a joy and a plaything, and is running to meet it like it ain't full of sorrows and troubles and sharp knives what can kill you if you don't watch out."

Esther tried to say something, but was not allowed to.

"Right now your eyes is shining like electric lights 'cause you done started to be a woman, and you don't know the first thing what it means. The Bible say a woman is a glory; but folks don't give a colored woman no glory, nor much respect. You got to fight for it all the way. Even then you don't get much." She changed the subject without pause. "I guess you knows by now you got to be careful about boys? You gotta get out them tomboy ways and start acting like a lady. And you gotta be careful."

Esther sighed inwardly. When Grandear started like that she went on and on. At such times it was best to look meek and grateful for instruction.

"I'll be careful, Grandear. I will!" Esther said. But it wasn't like her to dissemble. Involuntarily she knelt and threw her arms around her grandmother's waist and laughed up into her face. "Oh, Grandear, I love you so! I don't know why, because you fuss all the time. But I just love you! You don't need to be scared for me. Life isn't going to hurt me. Right now I'm so happy it's all inside me singing like bells. Listen, Grandear!"

She pulled the old woman's head down to hers, ear to ear, rocking her as she did. "Don't you hear the bells? They say, Ding, Ding, Ding! Esther Kennedy, you're going to be happy all your days, and your Grandear is the sweetest Grandear in the world!"

Her grandmother let herself be held for a moment; then

she withdrew primly. "Child, you're a caution, and that's for sure. What them bells is saying is Esther Kennedy better go back to bed 'fore she catch her death of cold. Besides, ain't you supposed to graduate today?"

"Yes, ma'am."

"Seems like since it waited so long, your womanhood could've waited one more day. Is you going to be all right? You don't feel weak or nothing?"

"No, I'm fine. Grandear, you coming to the assembly?"

Grandear said dryly, "Seems like I cain't get out of it. I got to see if you acts right on the stage. I hopes you knows your speech."

"I know it real well. And the social hour afterwards— you'll stay? Please?" But she knew as she asked that Grandear wouldn't change her mind about the social hour. She had promised old Pa Mead across the street that she would fix dinner for the grandson he was bringing home that evening, and Grandear never broke promises.

Lydia Jones said with some impatience, "Joseph Mead was my husband's best friend, and he has lived alone all these years since his wife died. He ain't had much pleasure in life. His one daughter what should have been a comfort to him was a disgrace to that good man. But she's dead now and I ain't going to drag for her. I just hope this boy she left turns out better. Anyhow, Miss Esther, while you's having your social hour, I'll be fixing dinner and cleaning up for Mr. Mead and the boy what's coming, 'cause folks cain't live in this world alone. So don't ask me no more, you hear?"

"Yes'm. But Pa Mead needn't live alone, Grandear. He could find a real good wife right here across the street."

"You full of the devil this morning, ain't you? That kinda talk could get you the switch. 'Sides, he younger'n me."

"Only four years. Anyway, you can't switch me today," Esther said, grinning.

"Don't count on it," Grandear said darkly, but her eyes twinkled.

On that day, Esther believed that it was her advent into womanhood and the fact of her graduation that made the day so special. But later it was to be remembered chiefly as the day on which she met Joe Mead. She would remember seeing Joe for the first time and the joy she carried in her all that day as being one and the same, cause and effect. Yet, on that day, she saw no connection between the two. In fact, she somewhat resented the coming of the boy, because it took the fine edge of excitement away from her graduation.

Lucy was more interested in the new boy's arrival. At the

suggestion that she attend the social hour in place of Grandear, she mildly, but firmly, held that she was more needed to help at Pa Mead's. For all her timidity, Lucy had a stubborn streak.

With no one of her own there, Esther found the social hour dull. Besides, by then she was feeling achey and lightheaded. She slipped out before it was over.

The recorded history of Leemouth, Alabama, does not tell how or for whom the town was so named. Whether there had once been a Lee family there, perhaps related to the revered Civil War general, or whether it was named in loving memory of some obscure English hamlet from which the first settlers emigrated, was not known. The town grew steadily in size and population until it reached proportions that almost, but not quite, made it a city. And at that point, it seemed to relax and cease expanding. For some forty years, Leemouth's area and population have been fairly static.

This fact has seldom distressed the city fathers. Leemouth's population is adequate to its industries, cotton and syrup. The town thrives in leisurely-paced, orderly living. It has long been the town's boast that no one in Leemouth is penniless—not even the Negroes who live in the section of town that is known as South Leemouth.

In the days of Reconstruction, the ex-slaves had been apportioned a then-isolated area of land on the town's least desirable outskirts. From time to time, as the town government set ample boundaries for Leemouth's growth, it invariably overlooked the simultaneous expansion of this area. At last, it became obvious that in three directions the Negro area had stretched itself to become adjacent to white neighborhoods. It could only spread outward then, which it did with rambling abandon.

Lydia Jones and her two grandchildren lived on the far outskirts of South Leemouth. Lydia's father had been farsighted enough to envision the growth of the Negro neighborhood, and he had bought a portion of land far from the other settlers at a ridiculously low price. He built two houses side by side there, for he had two daughters to inherit them. But one had died, and Lydia remained as sole heir. True to her father's prediction, South Leemouth spread out to encircle Lydia's land—but just barely.

With the land, Lydia also inherited her father's strong sense of property. No times were hard enough to induce her to sell. Although her husband Herman, a meek, unobtrusive little man, saw no good reason for paying taxes on an extra house, seldom tenanted, he made small issue of it, for he stood in awe of his strong, independent wife. When their only and late-born daughter Maggie arrived, Lydia turned to him and said in quiet triumph, "I always knew these houses would be for this child and her children! Ain't right for children not to have no legacy!"

The two houses were now to belong to Lucy and Esther, since their mother had died at Esther's birth. But the girls were too young yet to care about the legacy.

Esther had a place that was more hers—a small, flat-topped hill hidden away behind a tangle of bushes and trees, a five-minute walk from home. She had found it when she was nine, and laid claim to it by tying her handkerchief to a stick planted in the ground.

On one side, the hill sloped down a short distance to the railroad tracks. Esther never ventured in that direction. She had found a place on the near side where the first low-hanging branches could be pushed aside to reveal a natural clearing that led to the top of the hill.

She had discovered it by accident on a summer afternoon when Grandear was off on a case and Lucy was preoccupied with the sewing which was her talent. Esther had just started walking, and there it was—the flat, secret place at the top of the hill, hidden by many trees. She stood in the middle of it that first day, her heart pounding in her, and she said aloud, "This place is mine! This place is mine!" over and over again. She could look down between the trees and see her own house, but no one could look up and see her.

For her it was a magic place, to which she came only at special times. To come too often would be to risk the chance of others finding it. She would lie on her back in the deep grass, with the smell of wild flowers about her, looking at the sky. It was hers as nothing else had ever been. Not that she really minded inheriting all her clothes and toys from Lucy. It was right that Lucy should have things first since she was older and since she needed them more. Besides, sharing wasn't as easy for Lucy as for her.

Once Esther found a kitten, a puny, mewling stray; and Grandear let her keep it. But soon, because it was always that way, Lucy took to saying, "our cat"; and somehow, by and by, "my cat"; and after a while it was just another cat to Esther.

"Today is a special day," Esther said to the hill and the wind and the sky. "Today I started my womanhood and I'm out of grade school, and I'm happy."

She couldn't stay long, because the social hour wouldn't

last past five and Grandear knew it. She couldn't lie on the grass for fear of staining the white dress. But the excitement in her made her want to do something. She threw her arms wide and spun around in a circle five times and a half. "On my magic hill I'm wishing for my secret wish." Then she was giddy and had to stop.

The freight train tooted its whistle seconds before it came in sight. Still dizzy, Esther heard it and unaccountably it chilled her, the sad, weary sound. She hadn't truly listened to it before; at least it had never sounded like that to her before. She steadied herself and started to walk gingerly down the hill, her hands over her ears.

Grandear and Lucy had cleaned Pa Mead's house to a fare-thee-well, and the table, covered with Grandear's lace tablecloth, was laden with her choicest cooking. Pa Mead in his Sunday best greeted Esther at the door. He had been a big man in his youth, but his seventy-two years had shortened and shriveled him, so that his bald but still handsome head now seemed too large for his body.

"You got here just in time," he said to Esther. "We're just about to set."

He put a hand on her head. She loved him dearly, this old man so full of kindness and good cheer that was touching because it betrayed a hidden sorrow—or so Esther thought.

"How're you feeling, Pa?" she asked.

"Not too poorly, chile. The Lord gives me strength for each day."

The room was crowded with odd pieces of furniture, for it was living room, dining room, and kitchen all in one. The cot in the corner with the bright handmade quilt would be for the boy, Esther surmised. The one other room in the house was Pa Mead's bedroom. There was also a washroom with a toilet and a bowl, but no tub. Compared to the Meads, Esther felt that she and Lucy and Grandear were well off indeed. They had five rooms and a real bath.

"This here's my grandson, Joe. Joe, this is Esther, Mrs. Jones's other granddaughter."

Esther said hello to the boy. She eyed him with curiosity. Pa Mead must have looked something like that when he was the same age. But all that in the grandfather was merely big and benignly handsome had been chiseled in the grandson into a quicker, more sensitive version. At fifteen he was taller than his grandfather, but he was thin to the point of gauntness. Everything about him gave the impression of an

immense vitality, a contained power. His face, like his grandfather's, was unusual with its bold, distinctly Negroid features,
as evenly set as in a carving. Esther was especially fascinated
by his skin, which was a deep, almost translucent gold, and
by his ears, more perfectly shaped than any she had ever
seen.

But it was the boy's eyes which dominated his face, his
whole person. Dark and almond-shaped, they seemed to ab-
sorb and reflect every impression they received. Looking
into them, Esther had the curious feeling that she was being
drawn into kind, steady depths, and weighed there, and approved.

Grandear, at the foot of the table, was eying her sharply.
"You all right?"

"I'm all right."

Her grandmother nodded. "Today was Esther's graduation,
Joe. Next year she goes to high school. She's right bright for
her age."

Joe said, "Congratulations!" His voice was a surprise, deep
and resonant, a man's voice.

Esther wanted to hear him speak again. "What grade're
you in?"

But Pa Mead was saying the grace and there was no time
for an immediate answer. It was a long grace, in which the
old man thanked the Lord for life, health, sunshine, rain,
the food, the kind neighbors who had prepared it, and the
coming of his grandson. When it was over, Joe lifted his
head and answered Esther's question.

"I just finished the tenth grade. I got a double promotion
and skipped a year."

"I skipped one, too," Esther said, the strange joy catching
at her again, and this time surprising her.

Grandear said, as she passed the string beans, "Lucy ain't
so clever at books. She's just out of ninth. But the teachers
say she works hard, which is more than Esther does. Sometimes it's best for things not to come so easy."

Lucy's eyes were lowered, but Esther saw her smile,
briefly. Their grandmother was always quick to defend
Lucy, even when it meant disparaging Esther. It covered
her secret guilt at loving Esther more, and both girls knew
it and coped with it as best they could.

Esther said, "Lucy's real clever at sewing and keeping
house. I'm kinda lazy. Lucy can sew like anything!"

But for all the praise, it was obvious that Lucy would
have little to say. For the rest of the meal, the conversation
was between Esther and Joe, between Grandear and Pa
Mead.

That night in bed, Lucy was more articulate. "You sure talked your head off with that boy."

Esther was stung. "Well, you didn't have anything at all to say. You weren't even polite. You acted as if you hated him coming."

"I didn't want to be pushy like you. Seems like it being your first day and all, you'd have acted more like a lady."

"Talking doesn't mean I'm not a lady."

"Yes it do, when a person talks as much as you."

Lucy had been in school long enough to know how to speak correctly. But Esther suspected she said things like "it do" to provoke her. Esther cared about her speech, not for the reasons that it mattered to the teachers, but because she liked the sound and feel of words put together correctly, their sharp brilliance when given their full enunciation. When Esther corrected Lucy's grammar, her sister would reply: "Grandear speaks like that, and it ain't hurt her none. How come you got to try to talk so proper?"

The argument that Grandear never got past the fourth grade never seemed to impress Lucy. But Esther suspected that her English was better in school, at least in front of the teachers. Lucy believed in being a Roman in Rome.

"Lucy, why're you always mad at me?" Esther said gently. "I didn't mean any harm. Maybe I did talk too much, but it was such an exciting day. You know I started this morning?"

"I know."

"Aren't you glad for me?"

"Nothing to be glad about. Just a nuisance every month. Can't see why you were so anxious. I been suffering with it since I was ten."

Esther giggled. "You talk like an old lady, instead of only fifteen."

Lucy was silent. She was in one of her moods. Sometimes Esther sensed these moods were because of her relationship with Grandear. They both knew that, although Grandear was much softer with Lucy, Esther was her pride. The trouble was that Lucy was too eager to please ever to assert herself, too soft to stand up to the terrible Lydia Lucia Jones; and for this her grandmother felt a secret scorn.

It had been the same way with their mother. Maggie Jones took after her father. The only time in her life that she ever defied her mother was when she married Jackson Kennedy, the lusty, laughing, hard-drinking man, who, in spite of her mother's dire predictions, had captured Maggie's timid heart.

Jackson and Maggie Kennedy lived in the other house on the Jones property, a fact that the young bridegroom had resented, but borne with because Maggie would live nowhere else. From her position next door, Lydia kept a strict eye on the couple, dictating Maggie's housekeeping, and, when he was home from his travels, Jackson's behavior. By the time Lucy was born, Jackson's exasperation had reached the point where his drinking was worse and his trips home less frequent.

A source of further resentment was that he had fathered a mewling, sickly girl instead of the healthy boy he had expected. Maggie grew to fear him and his drunken rages more than she feared her mother. She died bearing Esther, and a few months later Jackson married another woman in another town and was seldom heard from afterwards except for an occasional check for his daughters.

Esther knew the story from bits and pieces of conversation that she had put together. But although she liked to think that her mother had died of a broken heart, she didn't blame Grandear. It was simply that Grandear was strong where her daughter had been weak. But Esther had inherited her grandmother's strength and will. She was Grandear's match; and because she knew this, she could love the old tyrant without fear. Grandear, in turn, who was unnaturally soft with Lucy, as though to compensate for her mistakes with the child's mother, had no such compunctions about Esther. Esther had no trace of Maggie, and Grandear could love her with all the harsh fire of her discipline, joying in the strength of this one that was like her, knowing she would not break nor spoil.

Sometimes Lucy could be flattered out of her moods, and Esther tried that now.

"Lucy, I've been meaning to ask you what you think . . ."

Lucy was pretending to be sleepy. "About what?" She yawned.

"Well, don't you think that since we're so big now and all, that Papa might decide to visit us soon?"

"Oh, Lord! You on that again! No, I don't think so. And you're crazy if you do. He never comes. Doesn't even send money any more. It's like Grandear says—he's no good. Besides, who needs him anyway?" Her tone was bored.

"I do," Esther answered involuntarily, and was sorry she had.

"Grandear and me ain't enough for you, are we? Next thing you'll be wanting to go off to him and his other wife!" Lucy was angry suddenly, and therefore tearful, as was her way.

Esther reached across the edge of the bed and caught her

sister's hand. "Now don't cry, Lucy. You know I didn't mean that. I just wonder about Papa, that's all."

"You ought to hate him for what he done to us all," Lucy sniffed.

"Oh, don't say that! You don't say things like that about your own father. Just let's forget it, huh? You know I love you and Grandear better than anything, don't you? Don't you?"

Lucy nodded, still sniffling.

"So, smile for Essie? One little smile?"

In the dim light, Lucy smiled. And to Esther it was, as always, a beautiful thing to see, transforming the thin, anxious face into something angelic.

Esther held her hand tighter. She said, "I do love you, Lucy!"

Then she yawned, and immediately fell asleep.

Chapter Two

THE SPECIAL DELIVERY letter from Susan Kennedy came the next day. Written in careful, stilted language, it said that her husband Jackson had died the day before of a kidney ailment, that the funeral was to be held on Tuesday, and that she was notifying Lydia Jones in case she wanted to attend with Jackson's two daughters.

Grandear snorted. "Kidney ailment, indeed! Like as not that there Jackson done drank himself to death. Now don't you two go getting upset about this. He ain't worth it."

Lucy had been unsure of what was expected of her, and was preparing to cry if necessary. Now she brightened visibly.

Esther said, "Don't you think we ought to go, Grandear?"

"I do not! We don't have that kind of money to go traipsing three hundred miles to no funeral."

"Then couldn't Lucy and I go?"

Lucy said quickly, "But I don't want to go."

"She has more sense, thank Gawd," Grandear said.

"Then, I'll go alone if you'll let me," Esther persisted. "He was my father. I want to see him before they put him in the grave."

Her grandmother rose in sudden trembling fury and stood over her. "Now you see here, Esther Kennedy. That man ain't cared if you was living or dead for more'n thirteen years. He went off and married his woman and left you two to me. I's raised you and fed you and schooled you like you was mine. It's me what wiped your snot and cleaned your mess when you been sick, an' I ain't paying no money now for you to go look at the evil, dead face of a man who ain't been no father to you."

Lucy said, "That's right. You ought to hate him."

Grandear swung round to her. "You keep out of this, Lucy. This here's between Esther and me." She turned back to Esther. "You beats the cake, and that's the truth! Good as I've raised you, you don't seem to know the difference between right and wrong."

Esther was trembling now, too. She stood up. "He wasn't evil! You were evil to treat him the way you did. He had a good reason to stay away. It's not wrong to want to go to my own blood father's funeral."

"Every man puts seed in a woman ain't a father. And it's high damn time you understood it, Esther Kennedy!"

"But—"

"I don't want no buts. You is hurt my heart today. Just understand that you ain't going, and that's all. That's all!" she shouted as Esther ran from the room.

Esther put the latch on the bedroom door to keep Lucy out. Grandear had said her say, and she wouldn't bother her for a while. She might not speak to her for a day or two—that was her way when she was angry. Esther could hear her in the kitchen singing a wailing spiritual, the kind she sang when she was upset: "I been scorned and I been 'buked . . ."

Esther looked in the mirror, wiping away the tears as quickly as they came. Everyone said it was her father's face, while Lucy's more regular features resembled their mother's. Esther examined her own high forehead, the wide cheekbones. The nose wasn't much of a nose. It was too small and snub. And the mouth was too wide and full, although her teeth were small, even, and white. But it was the eyes that everyone said were most like her father's. They were large and brown, with tiny folds of skin that crinkled the corners, as if they were always laughing under the thick lashes that curled up and sometimes tickled her lids.

She said to the mirror, "I don't even have a picture of him. That old mean Grandear even burned the pictures. It's not right! And here I was yesterday feeling so happy, and he was dead."

Esther wasn't sure why she was crying. She couldn't honestly love someone she didn't know. But if she'd known him, she would surely have loved him—and for this she cried. Although she wouldn't be at the funeral, Jackson Kennedy would not be buried without the tears of his own flesh and blood.

Later she went out on the porch and sat on the wooden swing. The boy, Joe, was sitting on the Mead porch. He waved to her. "Can I come over?"

She didn't want him, but she said, "I guess so." When he came, she said, "I guess you can sit here beside me if you want."

He looked at her. "You've been crying."

Esther bristled. He wasn't supposed to notice. "We got a letter. My father died." She spoke coldly.

"Oh. I'm sorry. Was he sick long?"

"Not too long."

"When did you see him last?"

Esther was angry. "Not since I was a baby, if it's any of your business."

The boy fell silent, and Esther could feel his concern. But she didn't care. She toyed studiously with the iron chain that held the swing.

After a while, Joe said quietly, "Well, at least you know who he was."

"What d'you mean by that?"

"He was your father. You know what his name was. I didn't have a father."

"Everybody has a father."

"Not everybody."

Esther turned to look at him. His face was expressionless, but it seemed deliberately veiled, withdrawn. She said in sudden sympathy, "Well, you knew your mother. Mine died when I was born. You had her all your life. I'm sorry she died."

He was silent again. Esther regretted saying it. She remembered that Grandear had said Joe's mother was a disgrace, whatever that meant. She changed the subject. "You like it here in Leemouth?"

He smiled at her then. "Yes. I'll like it more when I get a job."

"A job? You mean you're gonna quit school and go to work?"

His smile broadened into a grin. "No, I mean I'm gonna work so I can stay in school. I'll need books and things. I don't want to make it too hard for my grandfather. He's old, and his pension isn't much. Besides, I want to go to college."

Esther stared at him. "College? What for?"

"I want to be a doctor." He said it without emphasis.

Esther absorbed the idea slowly. The only people she knew that had gone to college were the teachers. She knew that doctors went to college to learn to be doctors; but since there were no colored doctors in South Leemouth she'd never given it any thought.

She asked, "How long will it take? I mean in college for you to be a doctor?"

"About nine years all together."

"Hey! You'll be real old when you get to be a doctor, huh?"

He laughed. "You're a funny little thing."

"I'm not a little thing," Esther retorted, sitting taller in the swing.

"Okay, but you're funny."

He was teasing her, and she didn't like it. It seemed that in spite of his friendliness, he thought of her as a child; and she didn't want to be a child any longer, especially to him. And that was strange. Grandear was right; what she needed was more dignity.

She asked primly, "When you've finished your schooling, you plan to come back here to be a doctor?"

"Sure. I couldn't just go off then and leave Pa."

She was relieved. "What made you decide to be a doctor, Joe?"

"Well, because . . . I just want to, that's all." His face closed again. He stood up abruptly. "I'd better be going now. I have to cook the dinner."

Esther laughed, shortly, because something about him annoyed her.

"What's so funny?"

"You cooking dinner."

Surprisingly, he agreed, and laughed too. "It's awful, too. What we need is a woman in the house. When you grow up, Esther, I'll marry you and you can do all the cooking. See you!"

He jumped the fence on his way out, his long legs clearing it effortlessly. Esther thought, "He's a real show-off!"

After dinner, Grandear said, "I suppose I ought to be more patient with you because of your age. At thirteen, girls is all glands and foolish notions. The medical books say so."

Grandear's "medical books" consisted of one ancient and tattered medical encyclopedia that she pored over every evening for half an hour as assiduously as she read the Bible for another half hour. The encyclopedia was the oracle of her midwifery and her care of minor ailments. Along with the outdated scientific methods, she also applied the "secrets" of which she was so proud, secrets that had their origins in Africa and had been handed down to Lydia Jones from her slave grandmother. On the matter of female functions and disorders, Grandear's vocabulary was an odd mixture of scientific terms and garbled folklore.

"However, I 'spects that no matter what your glands is doing, your mind ain't out of order. Therefore I hopes to get more respect out of you from now on, Miss Esther. Now go get the writing paper. Before I does my reading, we's going to write a letter to Susan Kennedy."

Silently, Esther fetched the writing materials. She knew that she would be expected to write the letter, for she wrote better than Lucy, and Grandear found writing laborious.

The three of them sat around the scarred dining-room table under the naked bulb hanging on a cord from the ceiling. Lucy, rapidly knitting a shawl, refused to look at Esther.

"Write, 'Dear Missus Kennedy,'" Grandear commanded. "Now say we got her letter and thank her for letting us know about Jackson's death. You got that?"

"Yes, ma'am."

"Now say we is not able to come to the funeral."

Esther looked up.

"Well, is you got that?"

Without answering, Esther wrote the sentence.

"But say we is sending a wreath of flowers by wire to reach there in time for the funeral."

Lucy's mouth dropped open. "We is?" she breathed.

"We are," her grandmother answered drily, watching Esther.

Esther wrote swiftly, feeling her grandmother's eyes, and punishing her by not looking up immediately. When she did she said meekly, "Thank you, Grandear."

"Well, I telephoned, and they said we could send one for about fifteen dollars. It's cheaper'n us going, and 'tain't decent for folks to be buried without flowers. This way we'll be sure he gets some. Now you sign that letter with all three of our names. Say, Missus Lydia Lucia Jones; then, Lucy Margaret Kennedy; then your name, Esther Ruth Kennedy."

Esther did as she was told. But although she addressed and stamped the envelope, she didn't seal it then. Later, when no one was looking, she unfolded the letter and added a postscript: Lucy and Esther are sorry their Papa died.

Chapter Three

EARLY ON A STILL morning in the heat of July, Lydia Jones woke her two granddaughters.

"Munsie Atwater is 'bout to have her baby. She's labored since yesterday evening, and it's 'bout time. She got no folks and no husband. This is her first and I 'bout will need help to bring it. Esther, you is almost grown now. If you wants you can come along. Lucy ain't never wanted to help me. She can't stand the sight of blood, and I ain't aiming to make her; you neither. But if you wants to, I'd appreciate it."

Esther leaped out of bed. She had never imagined that Grandear would ask her along on a case, at least not before she was sixteen or so. To see a real baby born! "I'll be ready before you know it, Grandear."

Her grandmother nodded. "Good. Lucy, you make us some coffee, and I'll get my things together."

Lucy followed Esther into the bathroom. "You mean you really want to go?" she asked incredulously.

Brushing her teeth hurriedly, Esther nodded.

"But it's awful! A whole lot of blood, and they screams and screams!"

Esther spat joyously. "Sure; because it hurts, until it's over. Anyway, there's not all that much blood."

"And you don't mind seeing people hurt?" There was reproach in Lucy's tone.

Esther paused in her washing. "Of course I mind, Lucy. But I'm not going just to watch. I'm going to help Grandear. Folks in pain need people to help them. But I do want to see it. There are two things I've always wanted to see—somebody borning and somebody dying."

Lucy blanched. "You're real peculiar, Esther. Sometimes it's not like we're sisters at all. I think it's awful to want to see people die."

Esther shook her head impatiently as she used the towel. "You never understand anything I say. I don't want people to die. But they do. Just like they're born, they die. And I want to see so's I can understand about it."

Lucy's face assumed a superior wisdom. "Understand what? Nobody understands why folks is born or why they die."

Esther had no answer for that. She said, "All right. You

better hurry and make that coffee before Grandear has a fit."

The soapy carbolic water was hot to the scalding point. Under Grandear's scrutiny, Esther did not flinch as she scrubbed.

"All the way to the elbows," Grandear commanded. "Use the brush on them knuckles and nails."

The woman lay on Grandear's sterile white sheet which covered the endless layers of newspaper that had had their time in the oven. The bed was narrow, and the woman was large. She was young, not more than twenty-two or -three. She wore the loose gown which was one of the many Lucy had made. Beads of sweat dripped from her forehead and she moaned with each periodic pain. Grandear had put a white cotton cap over her hair, and her round brown face under it was comic even in its contortions.

But Esther had no sense of amusement. Her excitement had given way to solemnity.

"That's enough washing, now," Grandear said. "Dry your hands on that towel."

The woman was sweating in earnest now. Although the windows were open, the little room was hot even to Esther.

"Should I turn on the fan, Grandear?"

"No. Best for them both not to. Just wipe her forehead. Hand me that padding on top of the pile."

Esther obeyed.

"The water is about to come," Grandear explained as she set the padding in place. As if at command, the water immediately gushed forth. Munsie gasped, and Grandear gave a small chuckle. "Right on time," she said, deftly removing the soaked pad and replacing it with another. "The child been growing and swimming in that water. Now it's so dry up there, it'll come out fast. You just relax, Munsie. That's it. Relax and breathe easy. Ain't going to be long."

Her voice was strangely gentle. She kept talking soothingly and reassuringly, while her supple hands explored the distended abdomen and adjusted the woman's elevated legs. But when the child began its descent, Lydia Jones stopped talking and concentrated on the expanding birth canal.

Munsie began to scream loudly and shrilly, calling on the Lord to save her. Instinctively, Esther caught her hands and began to talk in the same soothing voice that her grandmother had employed.

"You're going to be fine now, Munsie. There, there! It'll soon be over." Then, in sudden excitement, "It's coming! See, it's coming, Munsie! Breathe deeply now. Easy. Now push! Push!"

Munsie shrieked, and the child's dark head appeared. Esther caught her breath. In the next few minutes, she was conscious only of an overwhelming wonder.

Suddenly, the child was born. "Oh, glory!" Grandear breathed, and lifted her eyes to meet Esther's.

The moment was ever after to be etched in Esther's mind: the slippery infant, squirming feebly in the strong, gentle old hands; the panting, exhausted woman on the bed between them; the sweet, strong smell of the blood—and between Esther and her grandmother an empathy so sharp and clear that they were then not an old woman and a girl; only women, in that instant together, it seemed, at the heart of life itself, sharing a momentary but total understanding (deeper than knowledge) of what lay beyond all agony and ecstasy.

"It's a boy!" Grandear said to the woman. "A right fine big boy."

They walked home, silent most of the way until Grandear said, "You did good."

Esther took the praise without answering. She was afraid if she spoke she would lose the awareness of what she had seen.

Grandear chuckled. "Took me like that the first time I seen it too. Fact is, it's a glory every time I see it happen. Don't matter then that they comes into a world of trouble. Only afterwards you think about it."

"I don't want to think about afterwards," Esther murmured.

"Ha! Trouble is, most folks don't. Take Munsie now. I know she's lonely and ain't had much in life. She ain't got a kin in the world. But that don't excuse her taking up with a married man who got children by his own wife. Soon's Munsie got pregnant for him, he run out and left her. Now she'll bring this one up alone, or get to not caring and get more bastards than she can feed. If she'd thought about it, she'd have kept her dress down."

Grandear looked at Esther to see what effect her words were having. "Birth is a glory all right, but bringing children into the world with no father to provide for them ain't only a disgrace, it's a foolishness, and colored folks cain't afford it. Every time a black bastard is born, white folks nod their heads and say, 'That's how it is! Niggers ain't no better'n animals! They got no morals!' Not that *they's* any better—Lord, no! But they like to think they is. And I is saying this to you, Esther, 'cause every colored woman what holds herself up and lives decent is holding up for the race. You hears me, Esther? You cain't be black and live just for your-self."

"Yes'm," Esther said. But her mind was closed to Grandear's talk. It had happened, and she had seen it, been a part of it. And she would let nothing Grandear said now dispel the essence of her wonder.

Chapter Four

LATER THAT DAY, Esther tried to tell Lucy about it; but Lucy flatly declared she didn't want to hear such things, and ran her machine furiously to make her point. Esther decided to visit with Pa, because she was lonely. Grandear was out making her collections. That would take all afternoon.

No one in South Leemouth questioned how the long-widowed Lydia Jones managed to support her two grand-children. Births and minor illnesses were so frequent as to provide her a brisk trade. True, her wages for her midwifery and her nursing were minimum, but she was a genius at collecting them. She had no pity for inability to pay. Lydia Jones believed that meeting obligations was synonymous with making the effort.

"Folks what pays can respect themselves. Don't pay is won't pay, and won't pay ain't nothing but shiftlessness," she'd say in response to the most heart-rending tale of hard luck. "So I 'spects I'll take eight of them pullets now for my ten dollars." Or, "Since you say you ain't got that two dollars you owe me for tending to your boil, I'll just take two dollars' worth of them fresh vegetables you got growing in your back yard."

People who disliked having to part with fresh vegetables, livestock, and other negotiables always managed to fork up the specified amount without delay. If these tactics earned Lydia Jones a reputation for un-Christian extortion, they also accorded her a general respect and enabled her and her grandchildren to live in frugal comfort. Twice a week she made the rounds of her patients, and as often brought home produce for the table and money which would be carefully stored in the two padlocked tin boxes under her bed. Grandear had no confidence in banks. She had her own system of checks and balances, laboriously recorded in the large ledger, also kept under the bed. In the ledger were often to be found items like: Cured—Bud Fowler's influenza

—three dozen eggs; six bunches collards; one watermelon; and 50¢ cash.

Once an income tax investigator had called on Lydia Jones to determine why she had failed to file with the government and why she paid no taxes. On examining Lydia's ledger he decided it would be simpler for him and the government if they forgot she existed.

There were certain disparities in the entries that possibly only the old woman and her two charges knew about. While most babies were delivered for a fee of twenty dollars or its equivalent, there were a few that had cost less. Munsie Atwater's baby had been delivered for a mere five dollars. Sometimes, on making such an entry, Esther teased her grandmother with having, after all, a sympathy for the unfortunate. Then Grandear promptly shut her up with, "I charges as I sees fit, and ain't no business of yourn."

"Today I saw a baby born," Esther said to Pa Mead.

The old man was sitting on his porch, shelling black-eyed peas and rocking. He smiled at the girl. His full cheeks kept his total toothlessness from making a difference in his smile. Esther thought she preferred the lack of teeth to the false ones which he wore on occasions, and which made a clicking sound when he talked.

"So Lydia finally took you, huh? 'Pears like you'd do good in that kind of work."

"She said I did."

"That's good. You looking for Joe? He ain't back yet. He got himself a job, you know?"

"No! Where, Pa?"

"At the hospital. Cain't say as I'm much happy about it. They give him a big name—hospital attendant, they call him; but it ain't nothing but scrubbing floors and emptying slops. That place ain't fitting to be called a hospital. Could have got him a job in a store, but he'd set his heart on this."

"I guess it'll help him learn to be a doctor," Esther observed.

The old man paused in his shelling, his eyes proud. "I reckon. That boy's smart. Can be most anything he sets his mind to. And he's a good'un, not like his—"

He closed his mouth purposefully, and then continued: "Yes'm, he's a good boy and I'm right proud. Just like your Grandear's proud of you, little Miss Esther. And Lucy too, of course," he hastened to add.

Esther sat beside him and began automatically to help shell the peas. "When's he get off, Pa?"

"Ought to be here now. Chile, when he comes, get him to take some time to play. All he wants to do is work. Comes from that hospital and right off starts to clean and fix. Boy his age needs some recreation. Don't seem to cotton much to other boys."

"But he doesn't want to play with me. He thinks I'm too little. All he does is tease."

Pa smiled again. "After a while he won't think you's so little. 'Course he is more Lucy's age."

"But she won't talk to him. Lucy's real shy," Esther said.

He chuckled. "Shy is sometimes sly. Notice Lucy do come out on the porch when Joe's home nowadays. Notice too she be wearing her most pretty dresses. Yes'm, shy is sometimes sly."

Esther stared at him. It was true. In the five weeks that Joe had been there Lucy had changed, but subtly. It hardly seemed possible, but Lucy at fifteen was probably feeling and thinking things that she, Esther, knew nothing about.

There was Joe now, coming around the corner. And there was Lucy, coming out the door and wearing her best dress —the blue polka dot with the pretty full sleeves.

But the most incredible thing was her hair. Lucy had straightened her hair! Nearly all the colored girls in South Leemouth began straightening their hair by the time they were six or so. But Grandear strictly forbade Lucy and Esther to do it before they were sixteen. Grandear straightened her own meager grey locks on occasion, but she believed that hot combs and curlers would ruin the growth of her grandchildren's; so they had to content themselves with brushing and combing and experimenting with various styles of plaiting. For Lucy to stand there now so brazenly in her best dress, with her straightened hair framing her face in a becoming page-boy style was a rank defiance of her grandmother, the first Esther had known her to make.

"Your mouth's hanging open," Pa said drily.

Esther shut it, and then opened it again to speak. "She done her hair!" she exclaimed, unmindful for once of grammar. "Grandear'll kill her!"

The old man laughed. "Never thought she'd have the spunk. She do look nice, too."

Esther wasn't listening. Joe had reached her gate and had stopped to talk to Lucy. Lucy was answering and smiling back. Their voices were too low for Esther to hear from across the street. She felt a dim frustration. She had wanted to tell Joe about seeing the baby born, since he was going to be a doctor and all. But she had come over wearing the same faded old dress and the sneakers with the holes in the toes, so eager to tell that she hadn't even bothered to comb her hair. And there he was, not noticing her, talking to Lucy, who was all dressed up as if it wasn't just a plain old Tuesday.

Joe laughed, evidently at something Lucy had said, and Esther wondered why the sound of it upset her so. She shelled the last few peas viciously.

"Now you wouldn't be jealous, would you, Miss Esther?" Pa teased.

She looked at him. The eyes were twinkling, but they also held concern. This old man had been her friend ever since she could remember. "Yes, sir. It seems I am. But Pa, I've never been jealous of Lucy before!" She said it in puzzlement.

"Uh-hmm. Well, don't let it show, that's all. Will come a time the little difference in your ages won't matter. Don't you worry none."

But she did worry. Grandear hardly fussed at all about what Lucy had done. In fact, she conceded that the page-boy was pretty, and said that since Lucy was nearly grown anyway, the hot combs probably wouldn't hurt her. Esther was sharply warned not to follow suit until she got permission. "And that ain't for a long time yet."

Esther was tempted to tell Grandear that Lucy's sprucing up was for Joe's benefit; but Lucy looked so relieved at not being scolded that she didn't have the heart.

The thing that worried her most was that she really was jealous. Not about Lucy's hair—the momentary envy at that had been underscored by a pride in her sister's daring and the pretty results; it was the way she felt about Joe that troubled her. Why should she care if he paid more attention to Lucy than to her? After all, he was just a boy.

Unlike the other girls her age at school, Esther still didn't like boys much. Most of those she knew were stupid and awkward, and show-offs. She guessed the thing that made her like Joe so was that he was different. But she wasn't going to be pushy with him, she decided angrily. If he spoke to her, she would speak to him, and that was all. And she positively would not dress up for his benefit.

In the weeks that followed, she would see him going to and from work, or in his yard, hanging out the washing or tending the vegetable patch. Somehow he never looked silly doing woman's chores. He did them with a matter-of-fact thoroughness, with neither enthusiasm nor embarrassment. Occasionally he would walk over to talk with her in his casual, teasing way. More often he came to talk with Lucy. It happened that way because Lucy was more often on the porch when he was around. Lucy had taken to doing on the porch all the sewing that didn't have to be done on the machine. She'd go out just about the time for Joe to come home, claiming it was too hot to stay in the house any longer, which was silly, because the hottest part of the day was over by then.

Once Esther eavesdropped on one of their conversations. She was sitting in the living room and could hear them clearly.

"That's a pretty thing you're making," Joe said. "What's it going to be?"

"Just a dress," Lucy replied.

"I bet it'll be pretty when it's finished."

"Well, thank you!"

"You're smart. Most girls don't like to sew."

"I know. But I like it."

"I see you do. Gee, it's hot today!"

"It sure is. Seems like it's the hottest day of the year."

"Ain't that a preach!" Esther said half aloud, in disgust. It seemed to her that two intelligent people should have more to talk about than clothes and the weather.

But she was pleased. When he talked with her, it was about things that happened at the hospital, or the cases she went on. He was avidly interested in them. Sometimes they talked about school, the subjects they liked best, books they had read. It delighted her that Joe was a reader, although it seemed that their tastes differed. He liked books about science and history, although he admitted he also liked poetry and Shakespeare. Esther liked stories about people—the sadder, the better. She loved a book she could cry over. Joe didn't laugh when she told him that. He merely nodded as if he understood, and she was prompted to ask: "Do you ever cry, Joe?"

She asked it out of a sudden yearning to learn if he could feel the same way about things that she did.

He looked gravely, piercingly at her for a moment. "Of course," he said slowly. "Only not about things in books."

So her instinct that they were alike was right! But he had reasons she didn't know about for the strange, deep feelings in him—things had happened to him that had never happened to her, so that when he cried it was for real.

Later, when she pondered what had passed between them, she found that she no longer had any jealousy of his friendship with Lucy. But she would have to find a way to talk with him more often.

Chapter Five

IN THE REMAINING weeks before school opened, Esther went often with her grandmother to assist with delivering babies and attending the sick. She was, in Grandear's words, "a natural-born nurse" who reveled in her work. But it gave her less and less time to see Joe. Even the fact that Grandear had begun to pay her wages, in the same way that Lucy was paid for her sewing, a dime out of every dollar received, was not enough to mitigate Esther's desire to spend more time with the boy.

One Saturday, when Grandear was off collecting, Esther hurried through her chores and slipped out to the Meads. The preacher was visiting with Pa on the porch. Esther paid her respects dutifully, for the Reverend Sylvester Billingsley was Grandear's pastor too. He was a round, solicitous little man, young enough, but ponderous, and Esther didn't especially like or trust him. Still, she said what she'd come to say.

"Is Joe finished his chores, Pa? I'd like him to come with me, if you'll let him."

"Sure, Miss Esther. He can go. If I didn't stop him he'd do nothing but work." This last was pridefully addressed as much to the pastor as to Esther.

Rev. Billingsley mopped his brow. "And where, may I inquire, be's you taking the boy this fine morning?" His language was always grandiloquent, if appalling.

Esther kept a bland face and lied smoothly. "I have to go see about a patient for Grandear. It's a long way and she said I could ask Joe to go along with me."

Rev. Billingsley looked suspicious. "You helping your Grandear with her cases now, is you?"

Pa answered for her. "Oh, yes. Lydia say Esther is a real good little nurse. Joe! Come on out!" The boy emerged from the doorway. "You's to go with Esther here on an errand for her Grandear."

"Yes, sir," the boy said. But he looked his question at Esther.

"Where're we going?" Joe asked when they had turned the corner and the house was out of sight.

"To a special place I know. I wouldn't have lied about it, except that old nosey preacher was there. Anyhow, I

I promised Pa I'd get you out once in a while. He thinks you're working too hard."

Joe looked amused. "Suppose old Billingsley find out and tells on you?"

Esther shrugged. "How's he going to find out? Anyway, if you're scared and don't want to come, you can turn back."

He laughed his deep laugh. "Lead on, Macduff!"

"Huh?"

"Never mind. Where're we going?"

"You'll see."

"Why couldn't Lucy go too?"

"Why'd you ask so many questions? You think Lucy and I are twins?"

He laughed again. "No, indeed. It's hard to believe you're sisters." He was a most discerning boy.

"We're alike in some things," Esther said loyally. "You like Lucy a lot, huh?"

He scanned her face. "Lucy takes a lot of liking," he said gently.

They reached the entrance to the clearing, and suddenly Esther felt foolish. "There's a place in here. . . . Well, nobody knows about it but me. I found it long ago. I never told anybody before. But I thought maybe, since you like to read and all—well, maybe you'd like to come here too, sometimes."

His grave eyes looked through her again. Then he said, "You are a funny little thing."

"Shoot! You want to see it or not?"

"I want to see it."

"You've got to promise not to show it to anyone else."

"All right. I promise."

At the top of the hill, Joe stood still and looked. Then he threw himself down and rolled twice in the deep grass. Esther watched triumphantly. He sat up and pulled her down beside him. "Hey! I bet even God doesn't know about this place."

Esther laughed. "I reckon He does. Now that makes three of us."

He was serious again, pulling with his teeth at a blade of grass. "Why'd you want me to come up here?"

"I don't know. I thought you'd like it."

"I do. But if anyone knew they'd think it was funny."

"How you mean, funny?"

He broke the bit of grass roughly between a long finger and thumb. "You know what I mean. A boy and girl go off by themselves where nobody can see them, and people think evil."

Esther edged away from him. "It's you who're thinking evil," she said in a small voice. "It's your own dirty mind. I didn't even think anything like that."

His eyes were sad. "I know you didn't. In your mind you're still a little girl, even though you're thirteen. But people don't like to believe in—in innocence."

She was furious now. "I'm sorry I brought you," she said fiercely. "I thought it'd be fun to be up here with you. I'd planned how we'd talk about—well, about things. I figured you wanted to be friends. And now you've spoiled it, making out like I wanted to do bad things. And you're always saying how little I am, and making out you're so grown and smart. I just don't ever want to see you again, Joe Mead, and that's a fact!"

She started to run to hide the fact that she was crying, but he caught her wrists and pulled her down abruptly.

"You hurt me!" she cried. "Lemme go!"

He held her gently but firmly by both wrists. He said, "Don't, Esther. Don't cry. I won't hurt you any more. Just listen. Please, will you listen?"

After a minute, she stopped struggling and he let go of one wrist and began wiping her tears with his handkerchief. "I didn't mean to make you cry," he said, still holding to the other wrist. "I know you didn't mean anything by bringing me here. I was only worried about you. After all, I'm a boy, and I'm older, and I've seen and heard all kinds of things. I mean, I know how people think. Right now, if old Billingsley knew we were here, he'd want to make something nasty out of it."

"But how could he know? Nobody'll ever find us up here," Esther said, between the sniffs that were the remnants of her weeping.

Joe sighed. "Okay. I just wanted to protect you."

She removed her wrist from his hold. "I guess I should have thought about it," she said grudgingly. "I mean about what people would think. Only I didn't. Anyway, you don't need to come with me again. If you want, you can come by yourself now you know where it is. We'd better be going now."

He said, "No, we're here now. Does your wrist hurt? I'm sorry about that."

She was mollified. "Not now."

"What'd you want us to talk about?"

She considered. "Tell me some more about the hospital where you work."

"Well, there's not much to tell. You know how Wharton Memorial is—a great fine place, two big brick buildings—

and then over in the corner this little bitty building they call the Colored Annex. It's all right, I guess. Only it makes me kinda mad."

"Mad, how?"

"Well, you see these folk there, the colored patients, I mean, all crowded together because the place ain't big enough. It's bad enough for the grownups; but on the third floor where they have the kids, there's hardly room enough to walk between the beds. And then everything in the whole annex is second-hand."

"How come?"

He shrugged. "Looks as if the town thinks Negroes don't deserve any better; so every time something gets too worn-out for the white patients they send it over for the colored ones. It's not fair, Esther."

"You can say that again!" Esther agreed indignantly.

"Sometimes they send me over to work in the white building," Joe continued. "You should see the difference. Everything bright and shining. Esther, I hate white people, don't you?"

Esther thought about it. It was not an unfamiliar attitude. People around her were always saying with varying shades of feeling that they hated white people. Grandear herself implied it when she spoke of "them murdering white quacks" and the more general "white bastards." But to Esther, who had never in her life been closely acquainted with a single white person, it was a concept too vague to be adopted emotionally. Hating white people was to her much like hating the devil; something one said on principle, but without conviction, having but small actual acquaintance with either.

She said, "I don't know, Joe. They can't all be bad." Then, because it was her nature to prefer the tangible to concepts, she changed the subject. "Joe, what made you want to be a doctor?"

He took another blade of grass and began to chew on it. "I guess it's all mixed up with my—" He cut himself off.

"With your mother?" Esther asked softly.

He gave her a piercing, enigmatic look. "I guess you know all about that already."

"No. But you don't have to talk about it if you don't want to."

He shrugged. "There's not that much to talk about. She got mixed up with some white fellow when she was just seventeen. Her mother was dead and it was just Pa raising her. He was old to be her father, and he was sort of strict with her."

"Pa strict?"

"Well, he said it himself!" Joe said, with some impatience. "Anyway, when she got in trouble for this white fellow, she ran off to the state capital and got a job."

"And that's where you were born?"

He nodded. "But it was hard for her, not even finished school, and having me and all. After she had me she couldn't get a decent job, and she didn't have anybody to keep me. What I'm telling you is she got to be a prostitute." He spoke without passion, chewing his blade of grass and spitting out little pieces at intervals.

Esther waited, not looking at him, watching an ant nearby carrying a piece of stuff larger than itself.

"She used to try to hide it from me," he went on. "Nights when the men would come, she'd send me to the movies. I was nine before I found out. A kid in school just came right out and told me. We'd had a fight, and I'd beat the hell out of him. So he told me to get even. 'I'll get you,' he said to me, running all the time like a dog. 'I'd get a piece of your mother like everybody else, only I ain't got the money.' That's what he said. After that, it seems every day I had to beat up somebody for saying something like that."

Esther was holding herself still, watching the ant make its tedious progress to its hill.

"Anyway, that has nothing to do with it," Joe said, swatting at a gnat. "She was always kind to me. In fact, she was kind to everything. Used to spend hours chasing out a fly, rather than kill it. She did the best she could, Esther, you understand?"

She nodded. "It wasn't her fault, Joe."

"No. Maybe not." He began to speak now in a great monotonous rush, as though he couldn't help himself, as though his rapid vomit of words would empty him of whatever he was feeling. "Then, when I was twelve, she took sick. I tried to get a job to help out, but I was too young for more than throwing papers and toting packages. I couldn't make enough to feed us and pay the rent. She had something wrong with her heart. But she wouldn't stop what she was doing. Said she had to take care of me. She was going to a white doctor. When she'd feel sick, I'd call him for her and he'd come. Right away he'd come." He made a sound that bore some resemblance to a laugh.

He was in a half-sitting position, resting on an elbow with one hand flat, outspread along the ground. Esther killed the ant and moved her hand cautiously to rest beside his. He took the hand in his without seeming to know that he did, without stopping his flow of talk.

"I was pretty dumb in those days. I never wondered why a white doctor in the South would come so quick when a colored woman called. Always so nice he was, so polite. Till I came home one night and found them in the bed together. I tried to kill him. I was only twelve, but I tried to kill him, Esther. I hit him with everything I could find, and he ran. He ran like a dog."

He was gripping her hand, hurting her, but she didn't pull way. The pain in her hand made the listening somehow easier.

"The next day I went and found Ma a colored doctor. There were two in the city. I went to one and he was too old. He had the shakes and he was kind of dirty-looking, his office too. I didn't like the looks of him. The other one, Dr. Mitchell, was about forty. He listened to me, Esther. He didn't look scornful or anything when I told him about Ma. He just listened and that same day he came to see her. Afterwards he spoke to me like a man talking to a man; told me what was the matter with her, and what I had to do to help; how to give her the pills and everything, and how I had to make her stop being with men if she was to get well."

He took a deep, shuddering breath. "I did all I could. I worked whatever jobs they'd give me. But folks never had much for a boy that young to do. Finally Dr. Mitchell saw how it was and gave me a job in his office. He paid me a lot more than I was worth, I'll tell you."

He released her hand abruptly. "I worked so hard to help her, Esther. Oh, God, I tried! Three years I tried. But she wouldn't stop. Dr. Mitchell said it was a sickness with her and she couldn't help herself. I never believed that. It was as if she didn't care any more. And then she died. Oh, God! Why'm I telling you this anyway?"

He began suddenly to cry in deep, jerky sobs, and she reached out and took him in her arms, put his face in her lap, and rocked him with the age-old instinct of the female. "It's all right. I'm here. It's all right, Joe. I understand," she crooned.

"She never tried. For all I did, she never tried," he sobbed.

"It's all right, Joe. I understand. It's all right. I love you. I love you," Esther said, not knowing what she said.

After some time, he lifted his wet face and saw that hers was wet too, and full of his own hurt. He bent her head with his arm and put his mouth to hers, quietly, to comfort them both. It was for each of them the first kiss.

There was nothing said between them on the way home.

Nor did they touch each other again, not even with their fingers. But they walked side by side, and there was a peace between them, and around them the aura of reverence.

When they reached her door he turned to her. "Esther, it's because of him that I want to be a doctor. He taught me a lot of things those three years. He said I could be a doctor if I tried."

She said, "You will be, Joe. You will be."

And she went indoors, bearing her pain and her glory. At thirteen and a half, she had become a woman.

Chapter Six

ON THE COLD February morning that was Lucy's eighteenth birthday, her grandmother made her a present of the house that had been her mother's. Lucy stared in bewilderment at the deed now bearing her own name. "But, Grandear, what'll I do with it? You expecting me to move over there now 'cause I'm eighteen?" Anxious tears sprang to her eyes.

The old woman made a rueful chuckle. Lucy sure was good at crying with a loaf of bread in each hand! Lydia explained patiently. The gift was only to assure Lucy that her Grandear recognized that she was now fully grown. Grandear was concerned for her future, and had made plans for it. The house and land, and Lucy's share of the money that Grandear had saved, would make a good start for the girl after her graduation in June.

"You thought about what you want to do when you finish school, Lucy?"

Lucy shook her head vehemently, and her breathing began to be labored.

"Stop that!" Lydia Jones commanded sharply. "Don't be trying to have no attack on your birthday. You know I done long time prayed and doctored all that asthma out of you; so stop it, you hear!"

Surprisingly, Lucy stopped.

"Chile, you can't get yourself upset about getting grown," the old woman continued on a gentler note. "Not when I done planned so careful to make it easy for you. Esther will have a heap harder going, since she done set her heart on being a nurse. You say you don't want no career except your sewing; and that's fine, 'cause soon you'll be thinking about getting married to a good steady man what'll take care of you. And you two won't have no hard struggle to start out with, 'cause you got a good house and money enough for furniture and all."

Lucy burst out, "But I ain't planning on getting married soon!"

"Then it's time you start planning!" Grandear replied firmly. Her eyes narrowed. "I been afraid to say this to you, chile; but now I'm more scared not to." She paused; then spoke rapidly. "Lucy, Joe ain't for you. You *knows* it. Nature don't mate no lion with no kitten. Even if it was you he took to instead of Esther all these years since he came to South Leemouth, it wouldn't work. He's too strong, too fast-growing in his mind. Mind you, I ain't saying he's for Esther neither. I just know he ain't for you. And you got to get him out your heart and start thinking 'bout some of these other young men coming courting you."

Lucy's eyes widened in anger. "You're trying to shame me now, ain't you? I don't like none of those other fellows; but I ain't been hoping for Joe neither. Who said I was hoping for Joe?"

Her grandmother took her hand to stroke it, but the girl pulled away. "Besides, you make out all the time like you're so concerned for me; but all the time it's Esther you're thinking of. If I get the other house and land, who gets this house and land? Answer me that, Grandear! Answer me that!"

At this trembling challenge, a flicker of fear crossed the grandmother's eyes. "Nobody gets this house and this land until I die. And, be the Lord willing, I ain't aiming to do that for a while."

"But after you die?" Having gone so far, Lucy was not to be deterred now. She repeated, "But after you die?" And then she was frightened, because her grandmother, always to Lucy so powerful and fierce, seemed now to crumple and shrivel before her eyes.

Lydia Jones reached gropingly for the bedpost and eased herself into a sitting position on the edge of the bed. For the first time in her life, Lucy saw her grandmother cry.

"Oh, Lucy, Lucy! I weeps for you. Sometimes in my bed at night I weeps for you while I prays. You is so feared and jealous you won't let nobody love you. Your mother's house is good as this one. Got as many rooms, and as much land. Fact, it cost more because it's been fixed up more for the tenants. But 'cause you knows this one is for Esther, you wants it. Been jealous of her since she was born. Since you was little, I give in to you; give you everything the best; let you have your way; but it ain't been enough. I figured Esther weren't the jealous kind so it didn't hurt her none that I let you have the best. You even took her cat, a little old mewling thing you only wanted 'cause it was hers. And she never said a word, 'cause she love you so. Love you so she used to cry whenever I had to whip you. Lord knows I weeps for you, chile; for what is in your heart!"

"It ain't true! You always did love her best!" Lucy cried on a hysterical note.

Her grandmother grasped the bedpost and stood up again, the strength returning to her body. She made no attempt to wipe away the tears that had rolled down her cheeks. She spoke calmly now.

"If I love her best, it's because Esther has a heart what takes loving and gives loving. And I can't help it. Bible says, Deep calleth unto deep. I used to didn't understand what it mean, till it come to me that all folks got deep places in their souls what keeps calling out to other folks and hearing other folks calling out to them. It's what keeps us all kin to each other. Esther got a loving deep in her soul what can hear the deep in other folks and ain't afraid to answer. But you got yours so blocked up with jealousy and suspiciousness, nothing can get in and nothing can get out. All I prays for is, some day the deep in you and the deep in me will call out to each other. I never did try enough with your mother. I guess your father neither. And the Lord is punished me, 'cause I tries with you and gets nowhere. And it grieves me, 'cause I got a deep in me too, Lucy. I got one in me too."

She stopped, for she could see that Lucy had closed her mind now, refusing to understand what she was saying. She said gently, "Never mind now, Lucy. Never mind. You try to be happy on your birthday. I wants you to have joy today."

After a while, Lucy said irrelevantly, and with some satisfaction, "Well, anyhow, Esther ain't grown yet. I thank you for the present, Grandear."

Two weeks after her graduation from high school, Lucy Kennedy married Sam Adams. Sam was a carpenter, a big, phlegmatic, homely man with a genial disposition. He pleased Lydia Jones because at twenty-five he evinced a suitable maturity in his plodding industry and his single-minded devotion to Lucy.

He courted the girl with respect and persistence: respect, because he himself had never got past the eighth grade and admired everyone who had; persistence, because he saw his own size and strength as the logical protector of Lucy's dainty frailty. He loved in her a combination of small outward things: her delicate, even features; her constantly brushed, gleaming teeth; her immaculate ears and nails; the smell of soap and cologne about her; her prim rejection of all things gross and vulgar. Her very timidity was lovely to him, and in his efforts to please her he began to acquire some of her graces, taking on a neater appearance, modulating his booming friendly voice, the heavy thud of his tread. He would not seek in Lucy for more than could be seen. For all this, Lydia was pleased.

Esther, now sixteen and a half, was pleased also, because she liked Sam and because Lucy appeared happy. It did not occur to her that Lucy's decision to marry Sam had been made easier by Joe's being away much of the time at college. It had been a long time since Esther had linked those two together in her mind. Although they never spoke about it, she knew that Joe was hers, and she his, so naturally and inevitably that it never needed saying between them.

Lucy and Sam were married in the flower-decked living room of the bride's home, in the presence of all the neighbors and many of Lydia's patients. Esther acted as maid-of-honor, and Grandear, looking like an impudent bluejay in her blue satin, gave the bride away. Grandear had spared no expense for the wedding. After the ceremony, in which the Reverend Sylvester Billingsley rose to the occasion with many verbal embellishments, the guests sat down to a feast that had taken a week of preparation.

Lucy, having sniffed and trembled a little during the ceremony, was now radiant in the attention being paid her. She drank her grandmother's peach wine and chatted graciously, consciously pretty in the delicate white lace she had made herself. Sam beamed down at her with open pride, and everyone said they made a "right fine couple." When the time came for them to leave for their new home next door, the bridal party followed, laughing and throwing rice until they reached the gate. Sam scooped his bride into his arms, carried her up the steps and across the threshold, and shut the door.

Esther, feeling a little tearful, squeezed Joe's hand. "Wasn't she beautiful?"

"Sure was. You're sure she's your sister?"

She took a poke at him, and people nodded and smiled slyly at each other.

"Seems like you'll be having another wedding 'round here soon, Miz Jones," Munsie Atwater said, holding tightly to her squirming three-year-old.

Lydia snorted. "Ha! Them two got a lot of waiting to do. That boy got a heap more years of college, and Esther ain't even out of high school. I ain't better hear talk of no marrying out of them for a long time, and that's a fact! 'Sides, I cain't afford it."

They all laughed at that.

"I must say you done yourself proud today, Miz Jones," Rev. Billingsley said, patting his round abdomen expansively.

Several of the guests said, "Amen!"

"You's gonna be somewhat lonely, though, now that you's lost a granddaughter," Munsie said sympathetically.

Lydia laughed. "Lordy, Munsie! You sure do talk foolish. Lucy ain't gone nowhere but next door. Now you-all come back in for some more wine. Might as well finish it off. But by eight o'clock I wants you-all to git. Me 'n' Esther got a case in the morning."

"That one sure don't bite her tongue," a woman tittered.

In bed that night Esther felt a creeping loneliness. Lucy's bed, all smooth and made, looked unnatural in the darkness. Lucy was in bed now with Sam. Esther spent some time thinking about that. What kind of mating would that be, with Sam so big and clumsy and Lucy so small and nervous? She tried to picture them in bed together. She couldn't make them come together naturally in her mind. And she giggled, not so much at what she was thinking, as to ease the way she was feeling. Now that everything was over, she was suffering an almost unbearable tension. One night she and Joe would lie together, perhaps in this very house after their wedding. How would it be for them then?

Esther sat up in bed and threw off the covers. She bared and with her hands cupped her breasts, that were now the size and shape she had hoped for. It came to her that on their wedding night Joe would nurse at her breasts like a child. Men did that, she knew, not questioning how she knew; and, as if in response to her thought, her breasts felt suddenly heavy and sore under her touch.

Grandear coughed in her sleep and Esther hurriedly slid back under the covers. When her small, shamed panic had eased, she began to consider why it was with her and Joe as it was. From the first, because he was older and wiser, and because she had no weapons to fight that in him which she did not understand, she had let him set the pattern of their relationship. They both knew that when the time came they would marry. And because he willed it that way, they were moving toward the day with neither impatience nor sense of preparation. By tacit consent their embraces were brief, gay, light-hearted. Only in thoughts spoken and shared —probing, discovering, absorbing, delighting—only in this was their mating; and until the time came it had to be enough.

To Joe, the fatherless, the bastard son of a prostitute, fighting to achieve his own honor, to begin his line of ancestry with himself, love could only mean protection of the honor of the girl he loved—a spartan discipline of his young, lusty flesh. Esther accepted this, for she wished to please him in everything. But her hunger for giving was restricted only by his compulsion to virtue. In her own self-knowledge, she had been his for the taking, totally committed to him since that day on the hill. But that knowledge would shock and grieve him. Until the day when he considered it honorable and appropriate, she would have to wait—to give only what he asked—and that day was some eight years away!

It gave her some pride that they were not like most of the other boys and girls their ages who indulged in furtive affairs. It also gave her some pain. Joe had never once fondled her body, never touched her breasts. But sometimes, when he kissed her, she could feel his yearning, barely stifled. Then the holding herself away, the helping him not to betray himself—this was a knife in her heart, the kind Grandear said life was full of.

The midnight freight shrieked in the distance, and with the sound came an immeasurable feeling of loss—loss of Lucy, who had married and left her, and who had said no special sisterly word to her on that day; loss of Joe, the boy, whose soul had cried to hers, to Joe, the self-disciplined college man, with other needs greater than his need for her; loss of her own childhood with its simple, understandable desires.

"Silly, old, noisy train!" Esther whispered fiercely to the insistent whistle. "Why don't you shut up?"

Chapter Seven

ESTHER HAD anticipated that Joe would be free and at home for the summer after spending the school year at Howard University in Washington, D. C. He had chosen Howard because he could obtain his full medical training there. But to Esther's thinking, it was the end of the world. His letters often took three days to reach her, and they were few and far apart. He explained that he didn't have much time to write because he was busy studying and working his way through. Then when he came home for the summer, he got a full-time job at Higgins Drug Store and was free only on Sundays. Even during those afternoons spent with her on the hill, he was distracted, often poring over some book or other.

"Seems as if anybody who made straight A's all term shouldn't have to study all summer too," Esther reproached him.

"That's how I make A's, Friend," Joe answered calmly. He called her "Friend" as a teasing endearment, but she wasn't placated.

Esther was lonely. Lucy, all taken up with her wifely duties, seldom had time for her. Lucy was as enamoured of her new housekeeping role as a child with a new game, and the house next door was permanently spotless. Lucy now took in sewing on her own. When she wasn't cleaning or cooking, she could be found at her machine.

Grandear was lonely for Lucy, too. She had vowed that she wouldn't interfere with the young couple as she had with Maggie and Jackson Kennedy. But she refrained with considerable effort from taking the few steps next door unless invited. The strain of this self-imposed discipline showed itself in an unusual sharpness with Esther, who understood it, but nonetheless resented it.

It was unfortunate that Esther chose the time she did to ask her grandmother to raise her allowance. She reasoned that since Lucy was no longer getting a share, her grandmother wouldn't mind. Three years before, the allowance had been more than adequate. Now it seldom met her needs.

She made her request on an evening after a particularly difficult delivery, for which Grandear had had to call in a doctor. It always upset the old woman to need the assistance of "them murdering white quacks"—a resentment directed at the generally surly and grudging treatment given Negro patients rather than at the quality of the doctors' skill.

A case like that happened so seldom that Esther underestimated the duration of her grandmother's annoyance. When after dinner she made the mistake of asking for fifteen cents out of the dollar, instead of the ten she had been getting, Lydia Jones turned on her with unexpected tartness.

"What makes you think I'm made of money? You gets too much now for your trifling help. You gets not one cent more of my wages! If it ain't enough for you, go get yourself a reg'lar job."

Esther's argument that she was three years older and more experienced and efficient than when she started only made Grandear more obstinate. Grandear knew she was being unreasonable, but she was not one to admit readily to being wrong. And the argument ended with Esther saying huffily,

"Well, don't think I can't get a job." And Grandear answering, "And 'bout time you did, since you's grown yourself such expensive tastes. Sooner you finds out what it is making a living in this here hard world, better you'll appreciate all I done for you."

A week later, Esther began working as a maid-of-all-work in the home of Mr. and Mrs. Charles Miller. She did the cooking and light housekeeping. A woman came in once a week to do the washing, and another came periodically to do the heavy cleaning.

The Millers were a white middle-aged couple whose regular maid was on temporary leave caring for a sick sister. "We Millers are good to our help, Esther," Mrs. Miller informed her on her first day. "Why, I told Verdie to go right on up there and take care of her sister and those poor children. The thought of the trouble her sister was having was just about worrying her to death!"

Mrs. Miller was a lady of the old southern school. There was in her soft drawl a trace of flutter, and her speech was gently sprinkled with mild exclamations like Oh dear! My goodness! Well, I do declare! Everything about her—her features, her dress, her mannerisms—was soft, vague, feminine. Her only disfigurement was a visible goiter which, except for the artifice of high frilly collars, she refused to acknowledge, as she refused to acknowledge all things unpleasant or incorrect. It was a tenet of her religion that only that to which she gave credence was true. Therefore, her husband, a boorish man, was to her "a fine gentleman," and her moody, undisciplined nineteen-year-old son "a dear boy."

Esther found Mrs. Miller amusing and easy to please, and, with the girl's capacity for insight, she was not annoyed by her employer's unwitting patronage. Mrs. Miller could no more help being as she was than she could order herself to stop breathing. Negroes were to her a sub-normal species to be treated with indulgence as long as they "knew their place." Realizing this, Esther was careful to make no display of intelligence beyond that required by her duties. The housework was easy, and she had been cooking since she was nine and did it with ease and imagination. Mrs. Miller was amply pleased.

Grandear was less than pleased. "Fifteen dollars a week ain't worth the humiliation of being that white woman's slave. Ain't never thought no chile of mine would lower herself like that!"

"But it's only for a few weeks, and the money will come in handy for school clothes," Esther said.

"I is always bought you enough school clothes, Miss Uppity. Not so fancy as you'd like, maybe, but enough for you to go clean and neat. You is shaming me in front this whole town working in the white folks' kitchen. I don't like it at all, and that's a fact!"

"But Grandear, a little while won't hurt me!"

Her grandmother narrowed her eyes at her. "There's more ways of hurting than you know about, Esther. I's tried to shield and protect you and Lucy since you was born. Every time that white woman speaks to you like you's a shaggy house dog what only understands six words and ain't got no sense or feelings; every time she say, girl do this, and girl do that, like you ain't studying science and algebra and history and is due to graduate next year, and 'bout know more than she do since the teachers say you's got the highest I.Q. in the whole school; every time you takes what that white woman hands out, it is eating off a piece of your soul. Bye 'n' bye you forgets you is Esther, what is made in God's image, and ain't nothing left in your mind about yourself but what the white folks want you to see. And that ain't nothing!"

Esther opened her mouth and closed it. There was no stopping Grandear when she was wound up like that.

"I's tried to shield you. But you's hard-headed and I see I got to let you go your way. I thought you was like me; had my pride and spirit. But maybe you's like all the rest. My own husband Herman—your grandfather—he was a good man, a good painter, worked hard for the white folks. But he didn't have no pride, and they killed his soul 'fore they worked his body to death. They done it 'cause he let them. He didn't have no pride."

Esther had never heard such bitterness in her grandmother's voice before. She said gently, "I have pride, Grandear. It's not as if I planned to do this for a living. You know I'm going to college after I finish high school, and I'm going to be a real graduate nurse."

The old woman said nothing. Esther reached timidly to her and took the little body in her arms. "Grandear, I love you," she said. "And I know you love me. But you can't protect me forever. But if you want me to quit, I will. I don't want you to be unhappy."

Her grandmother's body relaxed suddenly. She said, "Chile, I'm a foolish old woman, what ain't got enough faith in the Lord or in you. You're a good girl and you're right sensible most times. Don't guess a few weeks in that kitchen will kill you. Colored folks needs all kinds of education;

makes us feel for each other. So, you want to stay, you stay. Only, chile, don't bow your head. You hear me, Esther? Most important, don't bow your soul!"

Chapter Eight

ESTHER SELDOM saw Mr. Miller. But what she did see of him she didn't like. She gathered that, among other business ventures, he was manufacturing a new type of syrup for which he had great hopes. He made frequent trips to other southern cities to try to push his new product. He had openly expressed ambitions to be the richest and most influential citizen in Leemouth, and liked to act the part. He was constantly critical of his wife's frugal habits.

Mr. Miller was a big, coarse-featured man with small and knowing blue eyes that made Esther uncomfortable. He had a way of speaking about her in her presence as though she were invisible.

"Must say that one's looks are a pleasant change from Verdie's," he remarked to his wife one evening when Esther was serving dinner.

"Esther is a pleasant girl," his wife agreed uneasily.

"A good cook too. They teach you cooking at school, girl?"

"No, sir. I mean, they teach home economics, but I learned to cook at home."

"Home economics, eh?" Charles Miller frowned. Then he laughed, slapping his thigh. "These nigra schools are getting real fancy lately. Home economics, ha? But it's cooking right on, ain't it, girl?"

Esther smiled gently, looking directly at him. She said, "As you say, Mr. Miller," on an even note, and the man reddened and slitted his eyes.

Mrs. Miller said quickly, "Charles dear, drink your soup. It's getting cold. You too, Paul."

Paul Miller at nineteen was a handsome young man, with his father's muscular frame and his mother's features made somehow bold and individual in his face. His mother adored him, and his father expressed his pride in the son he had sired by seeing he lacked nothing money could buy, and by treating him with a too hearty, man-to-man affection. Mr. Miller liked to think he and his son were pals. Actually, both he and his wife were somewhat in awe of the boy and had no understanding of him at all.

Paul had an outstanding scholastic record at college, and also excelled at football. For all this he had the envy and admiration of other boys and the adulation of the girls. He was nonetheless not much liked, for his was a mercurial temperament, as unpredictably capable of cruelty as of kindness. When he did not choose to be charming, he could be decidedly rude. He was given to long, inexplicable silences, and to sudden unprovoked rages which his mother sighingly described as the temperament of a sensitive soul.

Esther saw all this without much concern. She knew instinctively that, as a Negro girl in a southern white home, she must make herself and her reactions as unobtrusive as possible, particularly where the men were concerned. Yet, where she was simply repelled by Mr. Miller, she found herself reluctantly fascinated by Paul—by the contradictions in him. There were times when he spoke gently, lovingly, to those around him, for his every mood was an excess. At such times he was adored. He seemed to Esther like a snake, at once beautiful and evil.

Most of all, she was fascinated by the skill with which he used language. He spoke with the deft explicitness of the gifted; and Esther, who loved words well used, listened and absorbed.

For the first week or two, he hadn't appeared to notice her at all, hadn't acknowledged her presence. But on this day, after Esther answered his father so quietly, Paul looked up from his plate, his gaze taking her in as she moved unobtrusively to and from the kitchen. His eyes, brilliantly blue, were amused, curious, analytical, resting first on her thick black hair, which she straightened now, and which for work she caught and barretted into a neat single curl at the nape of her neck; then on her face, her neck, her shoulders, traveling the length of her trim uniformed body to her clean white sneakers, and then back again.

Esther was miserable under his scrutiny, and tried to stay in the kitchen as much as possible. But Mrs. Miller had a notion that her maid should be visibly at hand during a meal and she kept calling her back. Esther was clearing the dishes when the telephone rang.

"Oh, my goodness! I clean forgot! That's Ada Seabury calling me about the church supper," Mrs. Miller announced with her usual flurry. Mrs. Miller prided herself on possessing certain psychic powers, among which was knowing who was calling on the telephone. "You-all excuse me. Esther, you just serve the coffee for the gentlemen now."

"Yes'm," Esther said.

Mrs. Miller answered the phone in the library and called

out triumphantly that it was indeed Ada Seabury calling. Esther served the coffee with lowered eyes. But the look Mr. Miller gave Paul did not escape her. Back in the kitchen she could hear his voice. It was clear that he meant her to hear.

"Now that's what I'd call a juicy piece, ain't it, son?"

Paul didn't answer.

"Ho! Don't tell me she didn't take your fancy! I saw you watching her. Now, when I was your age—" He interrupted himself to laugh. "When I was your age, a good-looking colored wench like that wouldn't have been safe around me! 'Course, I'm not so spry now, but I've had my day. That kind got a fire in them to bring the man out of you. Yes, siree! Don't tell me you ain't tried it!"

"Don't be crass, Dad," Esther heard Paul say in a bored voice.

"Crass! Well, I like that! You just don't want to talk about it. I'll bet you've done your bit of nigger wenching."

"No, I haven't."

"All right, all right, if you don't want to talk about it."

"Talk about what?" Mrs. Miller asked, reentering the room.

"About why I don't want to join a fraternity," Paul said smoothly.

"Oh, that! Well, Charles, he must make up his own mind, mustn't he? Esther! I'll have my coffee now."

Esther was furious. But she hid it behind an expressionless face as she finished serving. After the fury subsided, she decided that maybe Paul wasn't so dangerous after all. Only spoiled. Only half bad.

She went home tired that night, and despondent. Grandear was right. The white woman's kitchen was no place for her. She would give notice the next day. But all she wanted now was the comfort and strength of her grandmother's presence, and the thought of Joe. What could hurt her when she had those two?

Lucy and Sam were having dinner with Grandear when Esther got home. It upset her to find them there. When Lucy and Sam visited, they stayed until bedtime. They had been married six weeks now, and Lucy wore her contentment with her married state like a sleek and satisfied cat, assuming the airs of a matron and being somewhat condescending towards her younger, unmarried sister. It was obvious to Esther when she entered that they had been discussing her.

"I guess you had your dinner in the white folks' kitchen?" Lucy said as Esther greeted her.

"Any harm in that?" Esther countered tiredly.

"Not if you like it like that," her sister said.

Esther was suddenly angry. Lucy was always criticizing and gloating over her these days. "I like it like that."

"Joe like it like that, too?" Lucy asked lazily.

Esther eyed her with scorn and addressed herself to her grandmother. "Any coffee left, Grandear?"

"Sure, chile. Help yourself. Sure you don't want to eat?"

"No, thanks. Just coffee. I'm kinda tired."

"Ha! Being independent ain't so hot, it seems," Lucy said to no one in particular.

"You let her alone now, Lucy!" Grandear said sharply.

"I ain't bothering her, Grandear. Just don't see how come she wants to work in Miss Ann's kitchen, that's all. It's not respectful to you. To us, neither; is it, Sam?"

Sam coughed to avoid answering, and looked miserable.

"I ain't saying I approves of what she's doing. But she's old enough to make her own decisions, and I figure we ought to let her be," Grandear said. "She'll find out soon enough what's smart for her and what ain't. She gets enough, she'll quit."

"I think it might rain," Sam said inanely. "You think so, Grandear?"

"I reckon you're right, Sam. My big toe been hurting something fierce!"

Lucy was not to be diverted. "You didn't let me make no decisions when I was sixteen."

"That's 'cause you wasn't able," Grandear said bluntly.

Tired of all of them, Esther excused herself and went to bed. She decided that she would stay with the Millers until their Verdie got back.

Chapter Nine

GRANDEAR WAS accurate in her prediction that working for the Millers would be an education for Esther. She was intrigued by the differences in their world and hers. The Miller house was itself a revelation to her. It was one of the older homes in Leemouth's most select residential area, its tall columns barely visible from the street through well-tended gardens and trees. Esther had not surmised the spaciousness, the actual number of rooms in such houses. She had not guessed that there were homes with a music room, a library, and a solarium.

But she was more fascinated by the people who lived

within. It seemed to her that in so gracious a setting it would be easy to live happy, gracious lives. She was acutely disappointed that it was not so with the Millers. It dismayed her that the instruments in the music room were untouched except for her dusting; the books in the library unread; and that no one sunned in the solarium. Mrs. Miller, for all her belief in "only the good," constantly wore a hurried, worried expression. She was active in a number of do-good projects, but they merely seemed to add to her harassment. Mr. Miller was seldom home during the day, but when he was, he seemed in a great hurry to be off again. Paul, apparently, was at home as little as possible. Early in the day he'd be off with his contemporaries, who would call for him with much tooting of car horns. On the rare occasions when he'd return early, Esther would hear him explaining to his mother that he'd had either a "mad time" or that it had been "a frightful bore." In such instances, he'd usually come in slightly drunk and highly voluble. Much of his talk was about a girl named Cynthia. Mrs. Miller would smile brightly and say, "Paul dear, you must be tired. Some nice coffee would be just the thing, wouldn't it?"

Most of all, Esther was learning the nuances of the southern white-Negro relationship. There were times when she was treated curtly: Esther, do this; Esther, do that—though Mrs. Miller was usually careful to add "please," it did not alter the tone of her command.

And there were times when Esther seemed to be recognized as a part of the family; at least, as an impersonal sounding board for family affairs. She grew to be wary of these times. Then she was spoken at rather than to, and was neither expected to listen nor to answer.

"My husband is a fine man, but he just won't practice gentlemanly ways," Mrs. Miller said to Esther. "Last night, my brother, Mr. Brookhouser—he's president of the bank, you know—he and his wife gave a dinner party. And all the important people were there—even the mayor. But my husband! Why, he was laughing so loud over some fool joke or other, he spilled soup all over himself! Just look at this suit! His best one, too! Did you ever see such a mess? Well, I hope it isn't ruined. It *isn't* ruined! I'm holding to the *good* thought!"

"I'll send it right off to the cleaners, Mrs. Miller," Esther said, understanding the strain of fighting vexation with good thoughts.

"It's a matter of breeding; that's what it is! Thank God Paul takes after my side of the family!"

Esther was not supposed to comment on that.

"Now I told that woman a hundred times, if I've told her once! I want her to leave my desk alone! Now where is that damn report? She been poking in my desk again, Esther?" Mr. Miller asked.

"I wouldn't know, sir."

"Where is she, anyhow?"

"She said she was going to a luncheon, sir."

"A damn luncheon, when I have to have this report! She's a goddamned scatterbrain, that's what she is!"

Esther was not supposed to comment.

"You know what, Esther?" Paul asked. He was quite drunk, and had difficulty getting the bottle of beer from the refrigerator. Mrs. Miller always hid the beer in the back of the box—to make it less visible, Esther supposed. "That Cynthia Hamilton is nothing but a synthetic bitch! That's all! A synthetic bitch!"

"Shall I fix you some coffee, Mr. Paul?"

"No coffee. Just beer. A synthetic bitch!"

Esther was not supposed to comment. It never occurred to any of the Millers that she heard or understood or judged.

Strangely, the whole business filled her with an almost merry excitement. It was as if she were able to see inside of them, but because she was invisible to them, they didn't know it. It was like being at a movie.

She refused acknowledgment of the other feeling—the deliberate hurt inflicted by being thought a nothing. She sensed that in that direction lay a deeper pain. But sometimes she detected in Paul, in his more sober and kindly moments, something that was different, a small interest in her as a person.

She was dusting in the library one afternoon, and because Mrs. Miller was out, she was doing a bit of browsing.

"Now, what interest could you possibly have in Emerson and his *Representative Men?*" Paul asked in a sarcastic drawl. He had startled her, and she turned to find that his eyes were smiling, curious. He had not been drinking, at least not enough to matter. He had a beer in his hand.

Normally, she would have evaded the question, but his expression prompted her to answer: "I don't know much about Emerson, except for a poem of his we read in school. I just happened to pick this up."

"You're fond of reading?"

"Yes."

"And what does Emerson say there?"

"Well, I don't really know. I just this minute opened it
[44]

when you came in. The first chapter is about the Uses of Great Men. He says it's natural to believe in great men." She had no idea why she was talking so. She seemed to have some need to make him aware of her.

Paul dropped carelessly into the nearest chair. She put the book back on the shelf and continued her dusting, hurriedly because she was flustered. But he wasn't through with her.

"And what do you know about great men, Esther?" he asked softly.

"Only what I read, Mr. Paul," she answered, her back to him.

"Oh, stop that foolish dusting and turn around!" he commanded. "I want to talk with you!"

She turned with a book and the dustcloth in her hands. She was nervous. It would not do for Mrs. Miller to come in and find them so. "What do you want to talk about, Mr. Paul?"

He smiled his languid, mocking smile, and sipped his beer. "The uses of great men, of course. I want to see what you think about. You do think, don't you?"

"I think."

"Then have you ever known any great men? At least one *you* thought great?"

"No. I don't think so," she said slowly.

"You mean you don't think of us here as great?"

She watched him warily. "No."

He laughed—a loud, abrupt chortle. "You're supposed to, you know?"

She didn't answer.

He said, "Maybe you know someone of your own people that you consider great?"

He was mocking her openly now, and she was angered.

"I think I know people who have a touch of greatness," she said carefully. "Maybe most people have a special thing in them that could be called great."

"Anyone in particular? Think now! Anyone in particular?" Under the mockery, there was in his face and voice a hint of earnestness, of actual wanting to know.

"Perhaps my grandmother," Esther said thoughtfully. "I think she has a touch of greatness. She's a midwife, and she's a sort of genius at delivering babies. I don't mean just knowing how to do it. I mean the way she feels about it, and about a lot of other things. It's in her . . ." She paused, searching for the right words.

"Soul?" he prompted. "You mean in her soul?"

She nodded.

His expression changed abruptly. He looked bored now; but Esther got the impression as he spoke that there was a violence of feeling behind the words.

"Don't you believe it, Esther. Man has no soul. He's just a rare combination of adaptive genes that dictate his needs and responses—an evolutionary cosmic blunder. Man is comic because he believes in the possibility of what for him is impossible—a personal integrity, directed by a personal divinity he chooses to call his soul. If man has a soul, it is no more capable of being upright than a toadfrog, and far less predictable."

He watched her as he spoke to gauge her reactions. She was conscious of this, but at the moment it didn't matter. Her brow furrowed in thought. "You're saying that man is not what he should be. But if he can understand what he should be, isn't it possible that he could be, Mr. Paul?"

His eyes widened. "Ah, touché!" he said softly. "Ah, touché, little black Esther with the laughing eyes, who I've always been told has no capacity for reason!"

She said, not knowing what else to say, "I have to start the dinner now, Mr. Paul. If you'll excuse me."

He let her go without another word, and somehow she was disappointed.

"I feel kinda sorry for him. He's all mixed up," Esther said. "Joe, why would a white boy that has everything be so mixed up?"

"Perhaps *because* he has everything," Joe replied. "Esther, I don't like you working there! I don't like the sound of this Paul. I don't like the sound of any of them. I wish you'd quit!"

"Well, it's only for another week. Verdie wrote Mrs. Miller she's coming back a week from Monday."

"Even so, I wish you'd quit."

It was a Sunday afternoon, and they were on the hilltop. Esther lay on the grass, looking at the sky. She was happy. It didn't really matter about Paul or the Millers. "Joe, recite to me!" she commanded. Joe had a large repertoire of poems that he would, on being much entreated, occasionally recite for her benefit. "Please!" she wheedled. "Pretty with sugar and cream, please?"

"What d' you want me to recite?"

"Do 'Who Knows?' "

"Why d' you always want me to do that one? It's such a sad thing."

"I know. But I like it."

He started softly to say the words by Paul Laurence Dunbar that most Negro children learn in school:

"Thou art the soul of a summer's day,
Thou art the breath of the rose.
   But the summer is fled
   And the rose is dead,
Where are they gone, who knows, who knows?"

Esther sighed, full of an aching content.

"Thou art the blood of my heart o' hearts,
Thou art my soul's repose,
   But my heart grows numb
   And my soul is dumb,
Where art thou, love, who knows, who knows?"

She turned to look at him, waiting as he finished the poem.

"Thou art the hope of my after years—
Sun for my winter snows
   But the years go by
   'Neath a clouded sky.
Where shall we meet, who knows, who knows?"

She opened her arms to him, and held him while he kissed her. When he tried to stop, she clung to him. She was a cup waiting to be filled; a door waiting to be opened. Her mouth sucked at his, and in sudden urgency his hands moved away from her shoulders down the length of her back, cupping her buttocks roughly and pulling their loins together, his lips making little sucking kisses down her neck.

She gave a small ecstatic moan, and he lifted his head to look into her eyes. "You know I'm hungry as hell for you, don't you?"

She quivered under his hands, unable to answer. Then he suddenly laughed and spanked her sharply on her buttocks, and said, "Let's go home, Friend. You're too young to be alone on a hill with a wolf like me!"

But she saw as he lit a cigarette that he, too, was trembling.

"Poor Joe! We'll never be able to wait eight more years," Esther thought, and wanted to cry with both sorrow and joy at that inevitable.

Chapter Ten

WHEN ESTHER returned to the house she found her grandmother in one of her oracular moods. The old woman was in the living room in the semi-darkness. She was sitting in the ancient rocking chair, its tall back dwarfing her small figure, rocking gently with the open Bible in her lap, and humming to herself: "You gotta walk that lonesome valley. . . . You gotta walk it for yourself. . . ."

Her eyes were closed. She opened them briefly as Esther entered, and shut them again. "Ain't nobody goin' walk it for you. . . . You gotta walk it for yourself. . . ."

Esther sat quietly on the sofa studying her grandmother's face, the face that at seventy-nine was still without wrinkles, and showed its age only in a tightening and sharpening of features—the nose, inherited from an Indian ancestor, now more hooked and beaklike; the mouth more tightly drawn. The girl noticed with a sense of shock that Grandear's hair was almost white. With her eyes closed, there was something witchlike about her, a deliberate mystic isolation into her own being. She was old. Some day soon she would die.

Watching her, Esther felt an unspeakable, creeping terror. It was as if before her eyes she was witnessing the old woman gathering her forces into herself, to make her lonely journey into eternity. Esther saw what she had never seen before—that Lydia Jones was lonely!

"My Saviour walked that lonesome valley. . . . He had to walk it for Himself. . . ."

"Grandear!" Esther half shouted it, calling her back, willing her out of that fearful insulation.

"Yes, chile. No need to shout. Where you been?"

"Walking with Joe."

"Ummm!" Lydia stopped rocking to peer at her granddaughter. "And the smell of your love is on you. And your trials. Come here to me."

Obediently, Esther went and sat on the rug at her grandmother's feet. The old woman began to stroke her hair, talking, almost it seemed, to herself. "Lord, how come this one is chosen for the waiting, what ain't fit for it? Lucy would have been more fit to wait—she what I done married off right away. Lord, if I just had the strength to see this one through! But You knows best. You knows best! Esther, how long is you had woman feelings for Joe?"

"A long time now," Esther answered softly.

"And he for you?"

Esther nodded. "But we don't, Grandear." She said it with a touch of pride, lifting her head to meet the old eyes.

"I knows that! I also knows it ain't your fault you don't, Miss Pepperpot! The Lord is give me one blessing that that boy is upright."

Esther caught the gnarled hands and rubbed her cheek against them. "Grandear, I'm worried."

"I is too."

"He's strong as anything! And—well, I'm not. Grandear, I don't know if I can wait till he's ready to marry me. Sometimes I almost try to make him take me. I'm ashamed, but I can't help it."

"You gotta pray for strength."

"I do."

Grandear began to hum again. "Ain't nobody to walk it for you. . . . You gotta walk it for yourself. . . ." She broke off.

"And that's a fact, Esther. You think I ain't walked it alone? Took my cross up early, and by myself I've walked it. I took care of a sick mother nigh on fifteen years after my father died. When I married Herman, I thought I could lean on him; but it was the other way around. All my life I is carried my load alone, and other folks' too. Soon or late, Esther, we all got to make it alone. A child born into this world knows that right off, and he cries 'cause he's afraid. We's alone till we dies, and maybe after."

Esther shivered. Someone was walking on her grave, she thought. Or Grandear's. She shivered again.

"Some folks tries to lean on others, Esther. They lie down in the road and lets others carry them a piece. But come a time even they got to get up and make it for themselves. Lucy will let folks carry her a long time. But you is made to walk on your own feet, to fight your own hard battles. Much as I loves you, I cain't do it for you. You gotta decide if the spirit is gonna get the victory over your flesh. And you is gotta fight the battle alone. Even Joe cain't help you."

"It sure seems an easy battle for him," Esther said resentfully.

Grandear chuckled. "Sho! He been fighting this kind since he been born. His Ma's ways taught him his lesson 'fore he could walk good. He seen what the flesh could do. Joe got bigger battles to fight. He ain't come up against the world and the devil yet. But he will, 'cause life don't give no letup. Soon's you win one, you got another one to fight."

"Joe will always win," Esther said tiredly.

"No, chile. He is weaker than you really, because he ain't got your understanding."

"What d'you mean?"

"I mean Joe thinks life is just working hard and doing right. But it's more than that. He don't understand that we's all mostly alike from the best to the worst, all put together on this here earth, and we cain't one of us make it alone. We got to go down that road feeling for each other. We's alone, but we got to stick together."

"Alone, but not alone. That's a contradiction, Grandear."

"No 'tain't! Trouble with you two is, *you* only understands the not alone part, and he only understands the alone part. One ain't no good without the other. Guess that's why the Lord put the love between you—so's you can help each other. Chile, I prays for you reg'lar. I feels my time running out."

There was nothing Esther could say to that; only to hold the hands tighter; only to cry out silently that that one thing she couldn't bear.

Chapter Eleven

ON MONDAY morning, Mrs. Miller announced to Esther that she was giving a buffet supper party the following Friday, and that Esther would be expected to stay and serve. Esther was excited at the prospect. It would be one more opportunity to see how the other half lived.

She helped her mistress prepare the menu. There were foods included that she knew little or nothing about, and, eager to learn, she asked questions about the preparation of such things as artichokes and pâté de foie gras, although the latter was to be purchased already prepared. Mrs. Miller was happy to enlighten her and went into much detail on the subject of certain delicacies and their origins.

The week went by in a flurry of cleaning, polishing, and waxing. Esther rarely saw Paul. When she did, he ignored her completely. If he remembered the conversation in the library, he gave no indication of it. Being not yet seventeen, she felt a small, unacknowledged hurt.

The party was held on the front lawn. A butler and an extra girl named Mary had been hired for the occasion. Mrs. Miller was in her usual anxious dither, and, unconsciously, Esther assumed the responsibility for seeing that things went well. "We're all right in here, Mrs. Miller. Don't you worry. Everything is ready, so you just go out and entertain your guests." Mrs. Miller gave her a look of mingled gratitude and embarrassment and left the kitchen.

Aaron, the butler, was experienced, and moved among the guests deftly, balancing the trays of cocktails. Esther and Mary followed with the hors d'oeuvres. Esther thought it was a beautiful party. The women in their soft pastels beside the immaculately white-jacketed men under the Chinese lanterns made the kind of picture she had seen in the movies and not thought real. She was interested that there were so many young people at the party.

She came at last to where Paul was standing, morose, scowling, a drink in his hand, a little apart from a group of six young men surrounding a girl. Cynthia Hamilton, Esther guessed immediately. She was all gold, this girl that Paul loved. Her hair, skin, and dress were gold, and even her eyes were more gold than brown, and she was exceedingly beautiful. Esther served her first, trying not to stare.

Cynthia's slender gold-braceleted hand hovered over the tray and then drew away. "You know," she said in a soft, laughing drawl, "it's in situations like this that I expose all the secrets of my psyche. I just can't seem to make decisions. Now what would you gentlemen suggest?"

What happened then astounded Esther. Six male hands reached immediately for an hors d'oeuvre, three of them reaching at the same time for the same piece. In the scramble the tray tilted and all its contents spilled in a confusion of bread, egg, cheese, anchovy, and caviar onto the slim golden chiffon folds of Cynthia's skirt.

"Oh, I'm sorry!" Esther exclaimed, in chorus with the six young men.

"Now look what you-all have done!" Cynthia said, on the edge of a scream. She collected herself instantly, and smiled, waving away the anxious handkerchiefs. "Now it's all right. Just leave it alone. I'll go clean up. Paul dear, would you take me inside?"

Esther was on her knees, cleaning up the mess, and anxious to get it over with and back to the kitchen. But she could feel Paul's anger. His voice was careful, deliberately rude. "You'll find the john first door to the left as you go in the hall," he said, turning on his heel and striding away.

Esther stood up to see Cynthia's great hazel eyes widen, then narrow. She said sweetly to his retreating back, "Why, thank you, Paul."

Esther moved away quickly, quietly.

Esther threw away the ruined food and sent Mary out with

another tray. Then she went to the powder room. "I came to see if I could help you," she said to Cynthia.

The girl was dabbing furiously at the spots with a towel. She didn't seem to notice Esther. "I'll fix him!" she said, rubbing viciously.

"Here, let me," Esther said. She wet a towel with soap, and slipping a dry towel between the taffeta slip and the chiffon shirt, began to clean the spots with long, even strokes. Then she rinsed them with another towel dipped in clear water. "Soon's it dries, nobody'll ever know," she said kindly.

Cynthia accepted these ministrations absently, impatiently, hardly conscious of Esther and her services. When the dress was clean, she looked down and smiled. "Well, you did get it all out, didn't you? That's nice. Thank you, girl. Next time be more careful."

"You're welcome," Esther said drily. But she was dismissed. Cynthia gathered up her purse, fluffed her hair before the mirror, and was gone.

Esther shrugged, adjusted the towels on the rack, and went back to the kitchen. It was time to start putting things out for the buffet.

Much later, when everyone had eaten, there was dancing on the lawn. Esther and Mary were in the kitchen doing the dishes and could hear the sound of the music and laughter from outside.

"White folks know how to have a good time; but only colored people know how to have a ball!" Mary observed.

"You got something there," Esther said, laughing.

"Now most of those folks out there are half drunk; but they still act quiet, even when they're staggering around. If this was colored folks, you'd hear them halfway round the town by now."

There was a lot of truth in that, but Esther didn't like the sound of it. "Not all colored people," she said.

"Well, most all. Except folks like teachers and so. Even they can get kinda wild. Of course, it's because Negroes have more feelings about things—their good times and their bad. White folks is cold. Look at the difference in how we acts at funerals. You ever been to a white funeral?"

Esther admitted she hadn't. Mary at seventeen was a philosopher, and it was no good arguing that it was more a matter of training than of feeling. She left Mary to finish the dishes and went into the dining room to see if anything remained to be done there.

She heard a murmur of voices in the library, and automatically looked at the great mirror that hung above the buffet table. The mirror was placed at an angle, so that when the sliding panels were open it reflected almost all the interior of the library.

Cynthia Hamilton was on the library chaise longue in the ardent arms of one of the six young men. She was giggling softly, and saying, "No, Pete! Don't, Pete!" as his hands explored inside the bosom of her dress.

Esther turned hastily to leave, and stopped short. Paul was standing behind her, also looking into the mirror. Their eyes met, his in a terrible fury, and hers in an enormous pitying concern. It was only long afterward that she realized it was at that moment she had made her mistake—in that moment when she had dared to pity him.

She edged away, and then almost ran back to the kitchen

Chapter Twelve

SATURDAY WAS Esther's last day at the Millers. She was glad to be going. There were too many undercurrents in that house; too much felt, thought, and left unsaid.

"You've been a good girl, Esther," Mrs. Miller said. "We're going to miss you. There's really not much to do today. Mr. Miller is away on a business trip, and I'll be gone all day, too. So here's your money, and after you finish the cleaning and putting away, you can go, too." She handed Esther an envelope. "I put in two extra dollars for your helping last night."

Esther had expected more, but she said, "Thank you, Mrs. Miller."

"By the way, Mr. Paul isn't feeling so well today. So about noon, you just take a little lunch up to him. Some of that roast beef would be nice."

"Yes'm."

"Oh, and Esther, you mind sorting the laundry for me? Makes it easy for the laundry woman. She comes Tuesday, and I don't want to bother Verdie the first day back and all."

Esther smiled. Mrs. Miller had forgotten she had told Esther that one of Verdie's foibles was refusing to do or sort laundry.

It was typical of Mrs. Miller's self-deceptions that, in spite of all she had left Esther to do, she still felt she was releasing her early. But Esther worked with a will, and by noon she had finished the bulk of her duties.

She carried the tray up to Paul's room with some trepidation. She dreaded facing him. She knocked at the door several times before he answered. She knew he was awake because his phonograph was blaring out a symphony. He was still in his pyjamas, propped up in bed, surrounded by magazines. A bottle of bourbon, half empty, stood on the table beside him. His blond hair was wild. He glanced at her idly as she entered.

"Mrs. Miller said that I should bring your lunch up to you," Esther said, not meeting his eyes, moving the bottle to make room for the tray.

"I hear you're leaving us."

"Yes, sir."

"Had enough of the Millers, eh?"

"Verdie's coming back tomorrow," she said, turning to leave.

"Don't go," he said softly. "Stay a minute and talk to me."

"I have things to do."

His tone turned wheedling, half-teasing. "What things? Now really, Esther! Don't tell me you're afraid of me!"

She met his eyes, the wicked mocking blue eyes under the tousled hair. "No, sir."

"Not even a little afraid?" He caught her hand, startling her. "Or maybe we just disgust you. Now tell the truth, Esther. Don't we disgust you?"

Esther didn't answer. He laughed sardonically, pulling her forward to look at her. "You walk around in your little white shoes and take us all in, in your little black head, now don't you, Esther? You look at my poor pitiful mother talking about only the good, and my stupid father trying to buy his way with money, trying to be a representative man—and you laugh at us all. Or maybe you're just sorry for us. That's it! You're *sorry* for us! Tell me, Esther, are you sorry for me? Tell me! I've always heard your people have big hearts—black skin, white heart!"

He was more sick than drunk, Esther realized; but she was past caring. She trembled from head to foot in her rage.

"I *am* sorry for you!" she said, snatching her hand away. "And for all your kind, since you want to hear it! Thinking white is right and can walk over everybody! Thinking everything is your due, and all you have to do is sit back and take, take, take! And you're not one of you worth a pot to piss in. And I'm more than sorry; I'm sick and tired of you all, and that's a fact!"

Then she turned, running down the hall, down the stairs. He caught her there at the foot of the stairs in the wide hall—caught her with the devil gone wild in his eyes—tearing the uniform from her body—tearing the cheap clean undergarments—stripping her naked—humbling her as they fought silently, her nails ripping the skin from his cheeks, his chest. And he said as he strove to enter her body there on the floor in the wide hall—said, hissing: "You are the pot that I'll piss in, little nigger devil!"

She began to cry as she fought him. "I'm sorry! I'm so sorry! Let me go! I never meant to say anything like that! Forgive me! Please forgive me!" she was saying, reaching desperately for something, anything to kill him with.

But there was nothing. Only his hard body with its unbelievable strength and intent. And he entered and took her there.

After a while she was mindless—only a body with its own instinctively willful purpose—making the urgent, agonized answering motions of coitus; while a small dim voice inside her cried ceaselessly, "Joe! Joe! Joe!"

When he was through, he lay for a minute stretched upon her, panting and spent. Then he lifted his head and saw her tears. And in his own eyes was a misery as deep as hers, as horrible. He said, "My God! You were a virgin!"

He gathered himself together, and left her there at the foot of the stairs, holding her torn uniform about her, crowding her shame into herself. He left her and went up the stairs, himself weeping, and not once looking back. He went up the stairs and vomited into the nearest toilet, and his loathing was for himself. A secret part of her, forever inviolate, knew this, noted it, stored it away for future pondering.

She put on her own dress over the torn soiled underwear. She threw the uniform in the incinerator, and she fled the house, running, running till she could run no more. Then walking, long miles, without heeding the distance, until she came to the hill. She took her pain there, and her despair, rubbing her ravished body with the clean grass, weeping up at white uncaring August clouds, hoping and praying to die there. But she didn't.

After a while, she went home, and was surprised to find that all that had been there before was still there. The little round clock on her mantel said that it was only four o'clock, and that surprised her, too. Grandear was still out collecting.

Esther took a bath and started the dinner. Only one thing had changed. From now on she was alone—alone with the thing that had happened to her. Grandear, Joe, no one could help her. For which of those who loved her could bear her shame?

You got to walk that lonesome valley. . . . You got to walk it for yourself. . . .

Chapter Thirteen

"GOD WILL NOT let me be pregnant," Esther went around saying to herself. She said it through September when she went back to school, and Joe, mercifully, went back to college. She said it stubbornly through October when her period still did not show. She stopped saying it on the first day of November when Grandear found her vomiting in the bathroom.

The old face went grey with shock. "Esther! You're pregnant! Oh, Gawd! Oh, Gawd! Oh, Gawd!"

The vomit was acrid, filling her mouth, her nostrils, choking her. She heard her grandmother's footsteps retreating gropingly to the living room, and her muffled wailing, "Oh, Gawd!" When she was able she went to her, and found her sitting rigid in the old rocker, with the Bible on her lap, silent now and motionless.

Esther sat on a straight-backed chair and waited.

After a while, Lydia Jones spoke. "Joe done this to you?"

"No'm."

"Who then?"

"The white boy where I worked."

"Oh, Gawd!"

"He forced me, Grandear!" When her grandmother said nothing, Esther cried out, "So help me God, Grandear! It wasn't my fault! He was drunk, and we were alone in the house. I took his lunch to him and we had an argument. And I ran and I fought. I tore up his face, but it didn't do any good. You gotta believe me!"

She sobbed for a long time. Her grandmother watched her, expressionless. Eventually she said, "There is one thing I want to know, Esther. I want you to look right at me, and tell me the truth. I believe he raped you. You ain't never lied to me. But did you fight all the time? Or, when he was doing it to you, when you was helpless, did you start to give it back to him then? Did you help him any at all?"

This was a horror not to be said. But there was relief in saying it—a cleansing. She bowed her head. "Yes, Grandear. I helped him."

"Did you have feelings for him? Did he mean something to you, this white boy?"

"I think I was sorry for him. He was unhappy, and sometimes he used to want to talk to me. But I didn't have feelings. Only for Joe. Only for Joe, Grandear!"

A long shuddering sigh shook the old woman. She said, "Esther, you was my one hope! My one hope!" And she began to cry.

After a long time, she lifted her head. "Esther, you start the breakfast now, and get yourself ready for school. I wants you to keep on going as long as they'll let you, you understand?"

"I won't be able to graduate anyway," Esther said miserably.

"Never mind that. When you gotta stop, you can finish by summer school or night school. You got to finish, 'cause now you'll have this chile to support and educate. You can still go on maybe two, three months. More you go now, less you got to make up later."

The child had no reality for Esther, but she agreed.

"I want you to promise two things," Grandear said. "I want you to promise with your hand on this Bible, that you will try to get all the education you was planning to get before this happened. And two, that no matter what happens, you will hold on; be strong! You got to be strong. And you got to keep on hoping and trying. Chile, no matter what, if you ain't afraid of life, someday you will taste and see that it is good! But you have to hope and hold on. Come here to me."

Esther went to her.

"Put your hand on the Bible and swear them two things."

Esther obeyed. But only to please her grandmother. Only to ease the pain in the old eyes. Lydia Jones seemed satisfied. She stood up and put her arms around the girl. "Chile, I wants you to know I love you. I is loved you more than life itself!"

That afternoon, Esther came from school to find her grandmother in bed. Lydia Jones never went to bed in the daytime.

"You feel sick, Grandear?"

"No. Just kinda tired. I been downtown all day. I'll get up now."

"No. You rest. I'll get dinner."

"Dinner can wait," Grandear said, getting up and going to the bureau to pull out a sheaf of papers. "I wants you to see this. I went to the lawyer and I done had everything made out to you like I did for Lucy. This house and land is

[57]

yours, all legal, so cain't nobody dispute it. I is named Pa Mead your guardian till you's of age; so if I dies, Lucy cain't do you no harm. You knows where your money is."

Esther was trembling.

"I is paid up my insurances. After my burial, will still be some left, and you is my beneficiary. Don't look so nervous, chile! I'm old, and no telling when my time will come. I just wants to be sure you is taken care of in your trouble. It's enough money there for you to hold on while the chile is little, and to get started on your education. By the time it runs out, you'll find some way to make it. 'Cause you won't have nobody when I'm gone.

"I went and told Lucy 'bout you when I come from town. I asked her to stand by you. But Lucy is always took things hard. She'll be bitter and hard on you now. You got to bear it. And you cain't expect much from Joe, seeing how it is. You know you cain't hope nothing 'bout Joe no more, don't you?" She examined Esther's face anxiously. "Chile, it's best for a long while now not to think about Joe at all."

Esther noticed that her voice sounded feeble. She said, "Grandear, you ought to go back to bed now. I'll bring your dinner in on a tray."

"Not right yet, chile. What I wants you to do is change my bed linens, and help me get a bath 'fore I lie down. And I wants you to look in that there drawer, and get me the new gown what Lucy made me."

It was all done: the simple ritual of spreading the sun-clean sheets, of bathing the frail old body, of putting on the new white gown. It was all done, not knowing, not wanting to know that she was helping Lydia Jones prepare for her burial.

When she brought the tray, she knew. Grandear was holding her hands to her heart and struggling for breath.

"Oh, God! I'll get a doctor!" Esther flew to the telephone by the bed.

"No!" It was a command, sharp and clear between the gasps, full of furious entreaty. Lydia Jones had lived without the aid of "them murdering white doctors" and would die without them.

Esther knelt beside her, sobbing. "Grandear, you've got to let me help you! You've got to let me do something! Let me call Lucy!"

The breathing was shallower now. It made a weird rattling sound. "Lucy?" The voice was small—distant. "Poor Lucy . . . Poor Esther . . . So hard . . ." She made a convulsive movement.

Then Lydia Jones said clearly, loudly, triumphantly, "Sweet Jesus!" And she died. Died while Esther watched. Died closing her eyes and her mouth in a great deliberate final victory.

Esther knelt for a long time there in the tremendous silence, in the still, implacable presence of death. And in the small room there entered unbidden a peace so great, so real, as to have for Esther the shape of light and the sound of wings. She began to pray in a whisper: "Our Father, who art in heaven . . ."

After a while, she got up and, beginning to weep, went to call Lucy.

Chapter Fourteen

SHE HAD labored too long.

"Esther, you got to let me call the doctor," Munsie pleaded.

"No, no doctor." She was two people: the one speaking clearly to Munsie; the other hearing the voices in her head. "No doctor," the first one repeated emphatically.

"You ain't but seventeen, but you're hard-headed as your grandmother was!"

You killed her! Same as if you stuck a knife in her heart, you killed her! It wasn't decent of Lucy to scream like that at Grandear's funeral. And she was starting on an attack of her asthma, too.

In the midst of life we are in death. Funny how the sweat popped out all over Rev. Billingsley when he preached.

"Jesus knows I don't know nothing 'bout bringing children into the world. And I got no license. If something happens to you! You got to let me call the doctor!" Munsie had no guts.

"I helped you bring yours!" Why was she speaking so loudly? "You just do what I tell you."

Lucy will do like I tells her. . . . You think life is a joy and a plaything, and is running to meet it like it ain't full of sorrow and trouble and sharp knives. . . .

"The pains coming faster, ain't they? Maybe it'll be all right now. How come you ain't hollering? Ain't no harm to yell when you's hurting. Screaming eases the pain."

You killed her! You killed her! Lucy was better at screaming.

Our children bring our grey hairs to the grave in sorrow. They breaks our hearts; but Jesus mends them! Rev. Billingsley squealed and shouted like a stuck pig.

Amen!

Amen! Jesus mends them! Even in the valley of the shadow He mends them!

You got to walk that lonesome valley. . . .

"Thank God! The water's coming! Won't be long now, Esther. How you feeling?"

Lucy, I've been feeling so wonderful today!

[60]

You killed her! Same as if you stuck a knife in her heart!
Thou art the blood of my heart of hearts. . . .
It's all right, Joe. I understand. It's all right. I love you.
I love you.
How long is you had woman feelings for Joe?
"Bear down now, Esther! You're doing fine. This baby is soon gonna be born."
In the midst of life we are in death.
Cain't understand how come Joe didn't come to the funeral!
I asked Lucy to write and tell him. Pa Mead was old and full of bewilderment. *Lucy, what did you say to Joe in the letter?*
Only what was what. That Grandear died of a heart attack 'cause she found out Esther was pregnant. Pregnant for a white dog!
"Bear down now, Esther! Push! Push!"
Bringing children into the world with no father to provide for them ain't only a disgrace; it's a foolishness!
Lucy and Esther are sorry their Papa died. . . .
There are two things I've always wanted to see—somebody borning and somebody dying.
You said you wanted to see somebody die. Now you killed her and seen her die! You satisfied? You killed her! You satisfied?
Don't carry on so now, Lucy! You'll make yourself sick!
Sam wasn't hard like Lucy.
She'll be bitter and hard on you now. You got to bear it. You got to walk it for yourself. . . .
"It's coming now, Esther. Hold on just a little longer."
Promise you'll hold on. Put your hand on the Bible. . . .
"Here it is now! Lord Jesus!"
Birth is a glory all right; but bringing children into the world with no father . . .
All that blood! And they screams and screams. . . .
Thou art the blood of my heart of hearts. . . .
Chile, it's best for a long while now not to think about Joe at all.
Did Joe come home this weekend, Pa?
No, chile. He wrote a letter though.
Pa, does he ever say anything about me?
What can he say, Esther? He's only nineteen and he's hurt bad. He cain't understand.
It's all right, Joe. I understand. It's all right. I love you.
It's best not to think about Joe.
The child gave an anxious tentative wail.
"Lord, Esther! This is as pretty a little girl as I ever did see!" Munsie said.

"You cut that cord carefully," Esther said, lifting her head.

"Right 'bout here?"

"Just a little longer. Yes, there. Now tie it the way I showed you."

"She sure is pretty!"

"Give her to me. I'll wipe her while you clean up." She took the child born in the bed where Grandear had slept, had died.

Took me like that the first time I seen it, too. Don't matter that they comes into a world of trouble. Only afterwards . . .

I don't want to think about afterwards. . . .

A child born into this world knows right off he's alone, and he cries 'cause he's afraid.

"There, there!" Esther said to the child. "There, there! Don't cry now! I love you." She was very tired.

I is loved you more than life itself!

"Esther, what you crying for? Now ain't no time to cry! It's all over. What you going call this pretty little girl born this fine May morning? I hope you's thought about it!"

You got to keep on hoping and trying. . . .

Thou art the hope of my after years. . . .

Esther, you was my one hope . . . my one hope!

"I'll call her Hope," Esther said.

And in Munsie's eyes there was a terrible compassionate understanding. She had named her own son Ishmael. Ishmael: outcast with his mother. Ishmael: God hears.

Chapter Fifteen

LUCY ADAMS had small faculty for self-examination. Even if she had been capable of analyzing her true feelings about her sister, she would not have been dismayed at what she saw. As far as her own emotions were concerned, Lucy believed that what was, was natural and therefore right and pre-ordained. She had always felt wronged and overshadowed by Esther, whose virtues she believed were few in comparison with her own. She had been restrained in this respect only by Grandear's blunt tongue.

Most of all, she resented her desperate childhood dependence on Esther. She had never felt safe in bed in the darkness if Esther was not in the room with her. Her person was secure at school only when Esther, formidably fearless before the biggest bully, was there to defend and protect her. Once a teacher had threatened to whip Lucy for refusing to recite in class. And Esther, hearing about it, had gone to the teacher and said, "Lucy can't recite because you make her nervous. And when she's nervous she gets sick. So you just better not whip her for that, because you'll have me to whip first!"

Esther's loving championship was a secret burden to Lucy; and when she married Sam Adams she felt a triumphant release. Now that she had Sam she didn't need Esther, and there was no longer any need to feign more sisterly devotion than she felt.

It was not that she didn't love Esther, she told herself. It was that Esther got far more praise and affection than was her due. Esther's charm seemed to hide her faults from people. But she, Lucy, would be guilty of no such blindness.

When their grandmother died in her disappointment and grief, the final reason for pretense was removed. To wail her accusations at Esther during the funeral was enough to bring Lucy the sympathy she had so long desired. She gladly suffered the worst asthmatic attack in her history before the face of all the mourning congregation so that it could be seen how wrongly their grandmother and friends had judged between them.

The worst thing was Esther's attitude. It would have been more like the Esther Lucy knew to be abjectly remorseful, or defiant and defensive. As it was, Esther was grave and silent, seeming neither to hear nor understand that she had fallen from grace—that it was due to her wickedness that Grandear had come to so shocking an end.

In the weeks that followed the funeral, Lucy listened tearfully to the sentiments of the neighbors: True, Esther had sinned and deserved every punishment, but it was not Christian that Lucy should put her away—should leave her to her own silent devices in the lonely house that death had visited. Lucy listened and began to see with growing satisfaction that here was a chance to reverse their roles. Where Esther was now helpless in her predicament, she, Lucy, could become her protector—a tower of resigned strength in her own securely wedded virtue.

She informed the neighbors that, according to Grandear's wish, she would "stand by" Esther to the end. And she went next door bearing gifts of chicken fried in batter the way her sister liked it, and a maternity dress stitched with her own hands. She sat frigidly in the kitchen, drinking coffee and saying, "After all, we're sisters. And I can't let you down, no matter what you done. But I just pray you can get a hold on yourself and act more decent in the future. You always been sort of wild."

Esther merely looked at her, silently, gravely; speaking when she did in calm and quiet tones, thanking her for the gifts. Esther had changed indeed, but not to Lucy's liking. Her irresponsible, irrepressible gaiety had been purified by disaster into a baffling serenity. She wore an aura of almost madonna-like purity; and the recognition of it startled and infuriated her sister. Esther in disgrace had no more need of her protection than Esther in favor. The one thing that Esther did ask, Lucy could not give.

"Lucy, whatever has happened, you're all I have in the world. Can't you love me anyway?"

For one brief moment something flickered in Lucy, yearned to say "Yes, yes, I love you." But the instant passed before she could bring herself to it. She could not give this one thing that Esther had always had too much of. She said, "Don't talk nonsense! We're sisters, and I said I'd stand by you." And Esther smiled slightly, returning to her solitary inward calm. At that moment Lucy began to hate the sister whom before she had only resented.

But she hid it well and continued to play her role. She visited often, and as often invited Esther to dinner. She presented her sister with maternity dresses and dainty things for the child to be born.

She had no intention of being on hand when the child was delivered, but she went over immediately on hearing the news from Munsie.

"How you feeling, Esther?"

"Tired, but all right now."

"Did you have a hard time?"

"No, I don't guess so. You want to see the baby? Her name is Hope."

"So Munsie told me."

Lucy had small experience with babies, but she had seen enough to know that here was an extraordinarily beautiful child, perfectly formed, its small face exquisite in sleep.

"It's a pity she's so light," Lucy said, watching Esther's face.

"Oh, she'll get darker as she grows," Esther answered with a trace of amusement. "Her hair is blond now, but it most likely will be brown; her eyes, too, even though they're bluish. That's true with most colored babies—the bluish eyes, I mean. Would you like to hold her, Lucy?"

Lucy took the infant gingerly, reluctantly. The baby yawned, clenched and unclenched a small fist, and then opened its eyes.

"Look! She's smiling at me!" Lucy exclaimed in astonishment.

"They don't really smile at that age, Lucy," Esther said drowsily.

"But she did! Smile again, Baby. That's right! See, she did it again!" But Esther had fallen asleep.

Lucy seated herself in the chair by the bed, carefully holding the child, not knowing whether or not she should risk putting her back to her sleeping mother's arms, or in the cheap cradle close by. She looked at the child, examining the petal-soft skin, the small, perfect features, and the first stirrings of maternal instinct rose in her.

It was right that she who was married should hold a child in her arms. She had been married a whole year and had not yet conceived. Was something wrong with Sam? With her? Could they have a child as perfect as this? Life was up to its old tricks again. No matter what happened, in the end Esther was rewarded and she was punished, or at least deprived.

A sudden tear rolled down her face and splashed on the baby's cheek. The child made a feeble whimpering protest. And Lucy began to rock it gently and to croon in a whisper, "Hush now! Hush now, precious baby! Aunt Lucy's here. Smile for Aunt Lucy. That's it. Smile!"

Chapter Sixteen

THE BABY was a month old when Joe came home for the summer. Esther was in the yard hanging up diapers, with Hope in her carriage nearby, when she saw him. He stopped his cutting of Pa Mead's overgrown hedge and stared at her. Instinctively her hand flew to her hair blowing about her face in the June breeze. She did not know that she was prettier than he had ever seen her, her figure in the cotton sunback full-blown to womanhood, her face alight with the peculiar glow that sometimes accompanies maternity.

They looked silently across the street at each other for a minute. Then Esther raised her hand in a tentative wave. He waved back in the same fashion, and then came over to speak to her.

"Hello," he said quietly.

He was too thin, she saw. "Hello." She had rehearsed this

moment in her mind many times, but now she forgot how she'd told herself to behave.

"You well, Esther?" His voice and manner were calm, remote. He could well have been talking to a stranger. But the tenseness she had always sensed in him was more visible now. At nineteen, he was taller, and gaunt as a rail. He kept biting his lip, a thing she'd never known him to do before.

"Yes, thank you. Very well."

"Is that your baby in the carriage?"

"Yes. Would you like to look at her?"

He looked into the carriage and remarked that Hope was a pretty baby. But he didn't touch her. Esther offered him a cold drink, which he declined politely. She asked about how he was doing in college, and he frowned and said that he hadn't done as well as he'd hoped that year; that it was hard, what with having to work his way, but that he expected to do better in his junior year.

After some more stilted and desultory conversation he said good-bye and went back to cutting his hedge.

She watched him go. It came to her that they had one thing in common: they had both learned to cover their wounds, to hide their hurt. She didn't talk with him at all again that summer.

During and after her pregnancy, Esther found herself with few friends left in South Leemouth. Lucy's proffered protection was patently exclusive of friendship. Many took their cue from the sister and maintained a disapproving silence. Some were merely indifferent. Some few, in honor of Lydia Jones's memory, were openly hostile.

Esther's attitude did not encourage improvement in this area. Had she shown any token of humility in her chastening, she would have been easily forgiven, like Munsie Atwater, who was only occasionally reminded that her son was illegitimate. But Esther went about her business, briskly indifferent to public opinion, treating friend and foe alike with the same distant politeness; and it began to be said that it was her money that made Esther Kennedy so uppity. Lydia Jones had made a mistake to leave all she had to that one. No one was certain how much money was left, except possibly Pa Mead, and he wasn't telling. People said that he was getting a little teched in the head since Lydia died. It wasn't like Pa to be rude, especially to someone like the preacher.

"Brother Mead, the Spirit tells me you need to confide in your pastor," the Rev. Billingsley said heavily.

"Reverend, I do my confiding in the Lord," Pa answered.

The pastor chose not to hear that. "It is well known, Brother, that you was Lydia Jones's best friend, God rest her soul! It is also well known that she left you to administer her estate until that unfortunate grandchild of hers gets grown."

Pa blinked innocently at him. "What estate? Ain't no 'ministering to be done to that house and land except to let that chile and her baby live there in peace. It's hers fair and square. Lucy done long time got her share."

The pastor said more sternly, "Now I know you's in sympathy with the girl, seeing as how your own daughter was once in the same predicament. But I appeals to you to be reasonable. That girl ain't in a fit position to handle that estate."

"That house and land don't take no more handling than it ever did," Pa said stubbornly.

Rev. Billingsley was exasperated. "I'm not speaking of the house and land," he shouted. "I'm speaking of the money!"

"What money?"

"What money? The money Lydia saved all these years, that's what!"

"Oh, you must be mistaken, Reverend. I wasn't put in charge of no money. Ain't seen none, so don't guess there was none." There was something of a pitying note in the old man's voice, as if he couldn't understand how a minister of the gospel could be so much in error.

Sylvester Billingsley controlled himself with difficulty. "Now Joseph, you know about the money. Like as not some thousands of dollars. Hear tell Lydia used to keep it in boxes under the bed. Only reason I guess it wasn't stole from her is folks around here had so much respect for her. But it ain't going to be like that with Esther. First one can get their hands on it won't feel no guilt about taking it, seeing she deserves her punishment."

Pa Mead nodded, his eyes half closed. "That's true, Reverend. I know many good people be liking to serve the Lord by robbing that poor chile. Now how was you planning to help them?"

The pastor was not sensitive to irony. He said, "I figure for her own good, Esther needs her money to be put in charge of someone she can trust."

"Someone like you, for instance?" Pa asked agreeably.

"Well, I probably am the best person, if I say so myself."

"Ummm. What's wrong with her keeping the money herself, if there is money like you say?"

" 'Tain't safe for a young girl to have money. If someone don't steal it, she'll 'bout fritter it away on a lot of foolishness. Else she'll let some smooth-talking fellow get it away from her. What she needs is guidance. I figure we ought to have a talk with her in the name of the Lord."

Pa Mead suddenly threw back his old leonine head and laughed long and gleefully. When he subsided, he wiped his eyes and said to the offended pastor, "See here, Sylvester. If you want to take charge of that girl's money, whyn't you just go over there and tell her so yourself? If she don't kick you out on your ass, she ain't Lydia Jones's grandchild! But don't figure on me helping you with none of your evil tricks in the name of the Lord. I stand by that chile long as I got breath! You hear me?"

The Rev. Billingsley, never having seen the gentle Mr. Mead so worked up, made a hasty departure. But the thought of the lone and sinful girl with all that money stuck in his craw.

Besides Pa, Esther had another friend in Sam Adams. During the lonely months while she had waited for the baby, Sam had stopped in to see her every day from work. Perhaps Lucy hadn't approved of this; but Sam was wont in his quiet way to do as he saw fit, whether Lucy liked it or not. He had come every day and done the heavy chores that Esther found more and more difficult. All winter long, he chopped the wood for the stoves; he cut the hedges, and trimmed the lawn.

"Why're you so good to me, Sam?" she'd asked one day.

He'd smiled his slow smile. "You're my little sister, ain't you?"

But it was more than that, and Esther knew it. In befriending her, Sam was doing what he could to make up for Lucy's attitude; to make up for what Lucy had done, and had failed to do. For Sam was a just man, who believed that good and evil are rewarded in kind. He did what he could for Esther's sake, but also because he hoped to avert Lucy's reward for her harshness to her sister.

Sam was slow of speech, and not clever; but he was capable of sound judgment, and Esther often found herself consulting with him, often turning to him for advice. It was due to his persuasion shortly after the funeral that she agreed to deposit in the bank the three thousand-odd dollars that Grandear had left her. She was hesitant about doing it, partly out of a superstitious regard for Grandear's distrust of banks, and also because she wanted to avoid paying the inheritance tax.

" 'Twill be better to pay the tax than lose all the money to some thieving folks in this here community," Sam declared darkly.

At the time, Esther didn't question what he meant; but she was grateful for having taken his advice when, two weeks later, the house was ransacked on an afternoon when she was shopping for her groceries. Esther was shaken. In all Grandear's lifetime, no one had ever attempted to steal from her. Now as soon as she was gone . . .

"You better spread the word, Sam," Esther said grimly, holding to her abdomen. The child was moving within her as if infected with her anger. "Let them know that nobody can get at that money. It's mine, and I intend to keep it. And tell all those church sisters who've been coming around here so often to keep themselves and their tin cans and causes away from me."

Sam grinned. "I'll tell them."

One day shortly after the baby came, Sam stopped in for a talk. "Esther," he said, "that money can't last forever. You and me got to sit down and plan exactly how you'll manage from this day on for you and the child."

And they had sat at the old table well into the evening talking and planning until Lucy came, angrily calling her husband home and denouncing Esther for keeping him; that is, she addressed her remarks about Esther to Sam, for Lucy always avoided open battle with her sister.

The plan was simple and practical. Esther was to enroll in summer school, get someone to keep Hope, and rent all of her house except Grandear's room, in which she now slept. The rental would give her a small income, probably enough to cover the expense of Hope's keep. That fall she would attend the State College for Negroes, which was located in the state capital, not too far away, and which was cheaper than any other in the state. The State College had an acceptable School of Nursing and Esther would probably be allowed a campus job to help cover her expenses.

Munsie, Esther thought, was the logical person to keep Hope. But Sam felt that Lucy ought to be asked first. Esther was rather dubious about it. In spite of Lucy's unexpected fondness for the child, she was no less bitter towards Esther, and Esther didn't like the idea of asking her for favors. She was taken aback when Lucy made the proposal herself.

"Esther, it won't be no trouble for me to keep her. Fact

[69]

is, I'd be glad to. You don't have no money to be paying somebody else."

"But Lucy, if you keep her, you must let me pay you."

"Pay? For what? That money got to stretch as far as it can, so's you can get your education."

Esther had a joyous flash of hope. Maybe Lucy was relenting towards her. She caught her sister's hands. "Oh, Lucy! You don't know how grateful I am! I've been so worried about Hope! You don't know what it's like knowing that you're all a baby has."

Lucy withdrew her hands coldly. "Well, it's settled then?"

Esther nodded, immediately subdued. Lucy was no more loving to her than before. She was merely doing her Christian duty. But she would be good to Hope. In fact, Esther was afraid, too good. Esther had never seen her sister as attached to anyone as she was to the baby, and it bothered her.

During the days while she was attending the summer session, her misgivings grew. There were little things. . . .

"Shh! She's just started on her nap. You look tired, Esther, and I know you got to study. How come you don't just leave her with me for tonight? Won't have to bother carting all that stuff back and forth, and you can get some rest."

All so innocent—so kindly—so valid. What was the harm, even when it happened oftener and oftener? Only some wild instinct in Esther protested this thing that was happening. But she had learned to be wary of instincts, and she said nothing.

"Where's Hope's little blue dress, Lucy? The one with the peacock down the front."

"Oh, that! It's getting kinda small. She's growing so fast! Anyway, she has new dresses in the bag there."

"Gee, Lucy! Five new dresses! Where d'you find the time to make all these things for Hope? I'm kind of scared you're gonna spoil her."

"Oh, shoot! You can't spoil a sweet little thing like that! Besides, she's just a baby and can't know the difference about dresses."

"That's what I mean," Esther said thoughtfully.

That night, and every other night before she went off to college, Esther took her child home with her; sang to her; nursed her at the breasts from which she would be too soon completely weaned; examined and kissed each perfect finger, each toe; crooned endlessly in the quiet of the night, "Mother's here, Baby. Mother loves you. And she'll take care of you. Don't be afraid, Baby. I'll never go away for long."

And when the child would gurgle up at her in delight, sometimes she'd weep a little saying, "If you could only understand why I have to go at all!"

At times like these, it would come to Esther that she was only seventeen; that she was alone except for the child; that she was desperately frightened. Then she would hold blindly as one shipwrecked to the one thing left to cling to —Hope's dependence on her. The determination to make a way for her child would rise in her, holding her impervious to the small gibes of her contemporaries in the summer-school classes, keeping her in calm separation from every intended unkindness.

The boys at school, knowing her history, often spoke to her knowingly, slyly. "Hey now, you cute little ole chick!" or "How about it now, Honey?" And wondered eventually how it was that she never responded. She didn't even seem to hear them.

The summer classes were attended mostly by laggard students making up for points lost during the regular term. These were the students who hopefully would receive a high-school diploma in August. Girls and boys alike were nonplussed by Esther's single-minded studiousness, and by her air of detachment from everything non-academic. By graduation day, they had all rejected her as she had rejected them, for she had never really been one of them.

Esther was happy enough that short summer term, for when school was out in the afternoons she could go home to gather Hope into her arms. It was at college, ninety miles away, where she often had to be away from South Leemouth for many weeks, that she came to realize the full weight of that small life that was hers to carry.

Chapter Seventeen

THE TRAIN pulled sluggishly into Leemouth, making creaky sounds, stopping for long minutes and starting again, as if reluctant to enter that quiet, unimportant town.

Esther pulled her two battered suitcases from the rack and began to make her way up the aisle. It had been a tiring trip. The train had stopped, it seemed, at every signpost and rainbarrel. Her back ached. She pushed through the protesting door and rested a moment in the open passageway, swaying a little to keep her balance, breathing deeply to relieve her lungs of the musty air of the car she had left.

"You can't stand here, Miss," a porter said, not unkindly. "You're supposed to wait till we get in."

She nodded and began the unsteady journey through the three unkempt, cheerless cars marked FOR COLORED ONLY. If she could get to the third one before the train stopped, she might get off by the station instead of halfway down the tracks.

One of her bags accidentally knocked against the feet of a man sprawled across a seat in a comic effort at a sleeping position. The man woke, glared at her, and shouted, "Why the hell don't you watch where you're going?"

Esther smiled at him and made a tired apology. The man grunted, and closed his eyes. Shortly after, she collided with a hard-faced, very black woman with a garishly red mouth, and with two fat hard-faced children in tow. Esther again apologized meekly. "Niggers!" the woman hissed at her in disgust, and Esther felt the urge to laugh, because the same word had come to her mind.

Then she felt two hands closing over hers, relieving her of both suitcases. "Let me help you, Esther," a deep male voice said; and her heart, like a wild bird just realizing its captivity, leapt and trembled in her.

It had been a long time since she'd seen him. Their eyes met, struck fire, moved away quickly. "Thank you, Joe," she said, letting him move ahead of her with the bags, his own making three, seeing as she followed only the strong taut lines of his body visible through the jeans and the blue polo shirt, moving easily, balancing itself against the lurches of the train; seeing the close-cropped hair, neatly trimmed above the golden skin of his neck, the tips of his perfect ears. She had half forgotten how she loved him . . . how she loved him. . . .

He put the bags down at the door and turned to smile at her, casually.

"I didn't know you'd be on this train," she said.

"I got on at Springville. You home for good now, huh?"

"I graduated yesterday," Esther answered; and the full meaning of that swept over her for the first time. It was over—the four grueling years. In her bag was a diploma testifying to the fact that she had earned a Bachelor of Science degree in nursing. No one could take it from her, this education that was Grandear's gift to her, this means of making her living. It didn't matter that she had only sixty dollars left. She had a moment of exquisite happiness, an ecstatic feeling of freedom.

"Lucky you!" Joe said with a grimace. "I still have two more years of med and an extra year for internship."

"You'll make it, Joe!"

He looked at her intently. "Of course!" he said simply. "We're two of a kind, aren't we? We get what we go after."

Their eyes clung again—searching. Then the train came to a sudden stop and the people behind crowded them out onto the platform.

"Hang onto me," Joe said, bracing himself and her against the push of the crowd, holding them firmly in check until the steps were put to the platform, letting Esther down first, and saying laughingly to the fat woman who was harassing him from behind, "Your turn next, lady."

They took one of the dilapidated old taxis FOR COLORED ONLY; and an air of gaiety hung between them. They talked in soft laughing exchange about things that ordinarily wouldn't have been funny; about one of Joe's instructors who lisped and frequently said, "Thith ith a thymptom to be notithed"; about the religiously fanatical matron in Esther's dormitory who constantly admonished the students to be "sumbeams for Jesus."

Eventually they spoke of Hope. Joe, it seemed, had seen quite a good deal of her in recent months, because Pa was ailing and the grandson had made his visits home more frequent. "She's a little beauty," he said. "Did you know she calls me Jojo?"

"No, I didn't." Esther felt an unreasonable stab of jealousy. She hadn't seen her child for four months. The last time Hope hadn't recognized her until Sam said, "Hope, that's your Mama!"

It was Sam who kept the word Mama alive. Lucy could not understand how the child found an absent mother more glamorous than a present aunt. Hope, a bright child, was quick to sense Lucy's resentment and baited her Tattie, as she called Lucy, with occasional outbursts of "I'll tell my Mama when she comes." From Sam's dutiful reports, Esther realized it was a trying situation for Lucy. There was some excuse for Lucy's refusal to speak of her to Hope.

"But it will be different now," Esther thought. "Everything will be different."

Sam met them at the door. "I didn't know exactly when you was coming," he said to Esther, kissing her on the cheek. "We kinda expected you yesterday."

"I stayed over to take the State Board exam. But it's all right, Sam. Joe helped me."

"Met on the train, did you? Well, come on in. You too, Joe. Lucy! Esther's here! Hope, come see your Mama!"

The child came running, and stopped short in the hallway, a sudden shyness drowning her eagerness. She put a finger in her mouth.

"Hello, darling," Esther said lightly. She opened her arms and waited the terrible moment till Hope flew into them.

After a while, they drew apart, searching each other's face.

"You're pretty, Mama!" Hope exclaimed, her eyes happily excited.

"You're pretty too, Hope," her mother said.

The child was just herself, having no salient feature that could be traced directly to her parentage. Her heart-shaped face with its delicate features was neither Esther's nor her white father's. Nor were the wide-spaced hazel eyes, the thick curly brown hair. Esther noticed for the first time that Hope's skin was almost identical in color with Joe's—the same bright, almost translucent gold.

But her mind didn't dwell on this. It was noting the stiffly starched blue dress, the blue socks, the immaculate white shoes. Esther had never seen her child in the slightest disarray. Lucy probably changed her clothes three times a day. It would be different now. Hope would get acquainted with earth and sun and wind.

"Well, you're home. You're most too thin," Lucy said. They embraced briefly, but Lucy's eyes were on Joe. "You two get in together?"

"Yes," Joe answered. "How goes it, Lucy?"

"Not too bad. You might as well come on back and have dinner with us after you seen Pa. He's been poorly today and mostly in bed. I took his dinner to him earlier, and I know he ain't fixed nothing since. I kept things hot in case Esther was coming."

Joe hesitated, looking at Esther. She was occupied with Hope and didn't turn.

"You better come," Sam urged good-naturedly. "Lucy's fixed ham and greens. And sweet potatoes and cornbread. Don't that make your mouth water, after that slop they feed you at school?"

Joe agreed that it did.

"You got a girl now, Joe?" Lucy asked during the dinner. "Maybe one of those taking medicine with you?"

"Oh, several," Joe said lightly.

"I mean a steady one," Lucy persisted, watching Esther's reaction. Esther and Hope were smiling at each other.

"Well, yes and no," Joe said. "There's a girl I like."

"What's her name?"

"Gloria."

"I'm his special girl. Ain't that right, Jojo?" Hope piped in her chiming voice.

"Say, 'Isn't that right,' Hope," Esther corrected gently.

"Okay. Isn't that right, Jojo?"

"That's right, sweetheart."

Hope jumped from her stool gleefully to run and kiss him.

"Ah! She's my child!" Esther thought sadly. "With my impulsive heart!"

"This Gloria—she's pretty?" Lucy kept on.

"Very pretty." Joe glanced at Esther. She smiled at him. He felt a certain pride that she would not let herself be hurt. "Nearly as pretty as Esther," he added on impulse, knowing that Lucy would be furious. Lucy was always obvious.

"Well, I would think anybody'd be pretty, not having to do anything but go to school and have fun all their lives," Lucy said peevishly. "Wait till she's been out making a living for a while!"

"Going to school wasn't exactly fun, Lucy," Esther said.

"Ha! I heard all about that campus life. I bet you been having yourself a ball! Lots of times I've thought about you, carefree, and going to this and that at college, acting like a coed; while I was home sewing and cooking and cleaning and looking after—" She stopped.

"Looking after my child? Is that what you were going to say, Lucy?" Esther checked her anger, seeing Hope's eyes widen, taking it all in. She said on a quieter note, "All you say about college is true. Only I wasn't part of it. Even if I'd wanted to be, I never had the time. You forget I worked my way through. I could never have done it on Grandear's money alone. Lots of times I've had to study all night to keep up. And Lucy, no matter what you think, I never forgot I wasn't like other college girls."

"How come, Mama?" Hope asked brightly. "How come you wasn't like other girls?"

There was a silence. Sam spoke before Esther could. "Because your Mama had to be extra busy to get through with school and come home to you."

Esther shot him a grateful glance.

"You better eat your dinner and stop asking so many questions," Lucy said. "Then it's your bedtime."

"But I thought I was going home with Mama tonight," Hope protested.

"Not tonight, Honey. It's too late."

"Now, Lucy," Sam began.

She turned on him angrily. "You just shut up, Sam!"

"I want her home tonight, Lucy!" Esther exclaimed.

"You realize it's ten o'clock!" Lucy flashed at her. "All

[75]

this excitement and late eating! I told you not to feed her any more. First thing you know, she'll be sick!"

"I want to go home with my Mama!" Hope was beginning to cry, taking advantage of the conflict.

"You hush, Hope!" Lucy, too, was on the verge of tears.

"I don't have to mind you any more, Tattie. My Mama's here now. So there! So there!" the child cried furiously.

"No, no, Hope!" Esther said quickly. "You always have to mind your Tattie, even when I'm here. It's very late, so I'll just tuck you in and sit with you till you're fast asleep. I'll tell you a bedtime story; how's that? And I'll come for you first thing in the morning."

The child stopped crying to stare at her mother in disbelief. Then she opened her mouth and began to wail in earnest.

"Now you see?" Lucy shouted at Esther. "Come on, Hope. You're going to bed. Right now. And no bedtime story either!" She took the child by her arm, giving her a little slap on her back when she resisted, and hauled her protestingly out of the room.

Joe was watching Esther across the table. She had started to tremble. He said, "Patience! It's bound to take a while."

"That's right," Sam agreed heavily. "Lucy's got so she thinks Hope is hers. You got to bear with her, Esther. She don't think straight like you. You could spend the night if you want. Then again, maybe it's best you don't, seeing how it is."

Esther nodded, not letting herself lean on their sympathy.

"Come. I'll take you home," Joe said.

Chapter Eighteen

JOE SET the bags down in the front bedroom—the one room in the house that Esther had reserved for herself. A middle-aged couple rented the rest of the house. They would be asleep by now.

Esther stood by the bed, all the past four tedious years suddenly descending on her. The house, the room, the bed where she had slept, all spoke of Grandear. Grandear, who was not there to welcome her, to exclaim over the scroll of paper in her bag.

"Is there anything else I can do for you?" Joe asked.

She looked at him, and tears came to her eyes, flowing

over. She stood before him, weeping in great silent despair; and he took her in his arms and kissed her on the mouth with a lingering tenderness.

She wept, still silently, with her mouth under his, until, sobbing, her lips answered his—her tongue—her teeth. She felt the male of him hard against her; and her own lean woman body was as strong as his in his maleness. They stood for a long time so swaying together in wordless passion.

She moved away from him at last, her eyes huge, brilliant, her lips swollen from his kiss. "You still love me!" she observed wonderingly.

"I can't seem to help it."

Their eyes held, hypnotized each by the other. His were black now, glittering. She had known this time would come; had deliberately chosen not to be totally cheated of him. She hadn't known when. But she was twenty-one years old. It was not too soon.

She began to free her body of the hampering garments, one by one, without haste, until she was finally free of them. He watched her until she was naked and waiting. Then he made a small moaning sound. "Esther! Oh, God, Esther!"

"Shh! Never mind now," she said, unbuckling his belt.

He was a bronze god, loosed from his control. She cradled his body in hers in her grandmother's bed; met his wild thrusting with her own fierce, forgotten yearning; gathering his soft cries of "Oh God! Oh God!" into her heart, her memory.

Tomorrow he would think, would reason, judge, blame them both. But tonight was her wedding night that had been wrested from her by one she hadn't loved, before she had reached the age of consent. Tonight of her own free will; she herself was her dowry. She was reclaiming her stolen future all encapsuled into one night. And she took her lover unto herself as the virgin peasant bride takes a husband— with joy and honor—without fear or shame.

Early in the morning before the sun rose, he got up and began to dress.

"I don't want an affair with you, Esther," he said grimly.

"I know."

"I never wanted that. If things had been different, we'd have married, in time. Now . . ."

Esther sat up in bed, pulling her slip over her head to cover her nakedness. She said calmly and sensibly, "Things aren't different, Joe. And last night doesn't change anything.

You needn't think of this ever again. I expect nothing of you. I know how you feel about me, about everything. I'm not trying to compromise you, you know."

He answered in anger. "You couldn't if you tried! I'm no damn virgin, you know!"

"I know. I recognized that." She hadn't wanted it this way on this morning. She would have preferred the things that had to be said between them to wait a while longer. But Joe, who had planned never to talk about it, would not have it so now that this had happened; and they armed themselves with their separate truths, to thrust, to cut at the dark festering that each had inflicted on the other—to draw blood—he in anger, and she in kindness.

"Yes, you would recognize it, wouldn't you?" He had paused in his dressing, and was standing in his shorts at the foot of the bed, his face cruelly casual. "You were always good at looking inside me, Esther. I guess you were often pretty amused at what you saw."

"I never was amused by you, Joe."

"Well, that's funny! I look back now and laugh sometimes myself! For a boy—a Negro boy, at that—I was really the one, wasn't I? You and I were so special, I thought. Saving ourselves for each other on our wedding night. Ha!"

"We wouldn't have managed that anyway," Esther said. "We had too long to wait."

"But, you see, I didn't know that," he said on the same sardonic, casual note. "I was the kind of simpleton that had to go to school to learn the practical facts of life. I had a good teacher."

She said nothing.

"I learned it all in one night, though. The day I got Lucy's letter, I simply went out with the first girl that was willing. In fact, I laid that poor chick every night after that for a week." He laughed, a short explosive sound. "I guess I'd have screwed myself to hell, if she hadn't got so worn out she wouldn't see me at all after that. The poor chick was frightened of me—thought I was nuts or something. Each night I'd try to make up for all those years I'd held off. And I'd bawl all the while—screwing and crying. Scared the wits out of her!" He laughed again.

She was cold, cold. "Lucy didn't tell the truth."

"Oh, no!" Joe said. "You underestimate Lucy. She told the truth all right. She acknowledged Paul Miller took advantage of you. Lucy told me. Sam told me. Pa told me. I've heard it and heard it! You were so innocent! We all know you couldn't help being raped by that white boy! I understand all right. He raped you like some white boy raped my mother when she got me. You couldn't help it any more than she could. It wasn't your fault when we all begged you to quit that job! It doesn't matter now, of course. I long time gave up mixing tears with sex." He began to put on his pants.

"Even if you blamed me, it seems you'd have forgiven me by now, Joe. It's been four years. But you can't, can you? Not any more than you've ever forgiven your mother."

He looked at her tiredly. "Sugar, I forgive you. It's your life, isn't it? You notice I haven't tried to give you a hard time. We can still be friends, if you wish. But as far as love goes, and this other—I just don't want any part of you, that's all."

"Can you help yourself?" she asked, wanting for the first time to hurt him.

He was better at it than she. He said quietly, "Esther, I'm not a child any more. And the kind of trick you pulled tonight—well, it won't happen again. I want you to understand that."

She said coldly, "I don't want it to, either. I do have some pride, you know. Besides, tonight wasn't exactly all my fault."

"No? Maybe not. I got the feeling you'd planned it."

She would speak the whole truth now. "Not especially for tonight, Joe. But I knew if you wanted me, I'd have you. I had to have you, because I love you. I've always loved you, no matter what you think." She saw the pained, desperate thing in his eyes and added softly, "Right or wrong, I had to have you."

"Like you had to have Hope's father?"

"Must you try so hard to hurt me, Joe?" she asked sadly. "No, I guess not."

He finished his dressing, silently, hurriedly. And he left her with hardly another word. But her body still throbbed and ached from his passion. His smell was in her skin, her hair. She willed her mind to close against the things that had been said. Later she would make her peace with them. Now, she would hold him a little while longer. She smiled, and slept quietly.

Chapter Nineteen

THE DIRECTOR of Nurses turned the credentials over in her hands. Her keen grey eyes took Esther in and gave no indication of their findings. Her whole appearance was compact, straightforward.

"With a brilliant record like this, you could go anywhere. Why do you want to work here at Wharton Memorial? Why, for instance, not at the county clinic? The pay is better, you know."

"I know, Miss Head. But I believe I'm more needed here. Any practical nurse can give inoculations and lectures on hygiene. And you don't have a single graduate Negro nurse at Wharton, do you?"

"No, we don't." The grey eyes twinkled briefly. "So you're dedicated to your profession and your people, eh? Well, don't look so embarrassed, girl! Dedication is a good thing in a nurse. The one thing that bothers me is that I've seen so many young women with the same look in their eyes when they start. They lose it so soon." She sighed. "You're about twenty?"

"Twenty-one."

"Well, you can give it a try. Tomorrow morning? The eight-to-four shift."

"That'll be fine," Esther said. "Thank you."

Miss Head ran a pencil through her short salt-and-pepper hair. "Don't thank me so soon. Have you seen what it's like in the colored annex?"

"Yes. I've seen it."

"What do you think of it?"

Esther liked this woman at first sight. She spoke without hesitation. "I've wondered why nobody tries to make improvements there."

Miss Head made a sort of snort and stood up, moving away from the desk to the window. "Don't you think I haven't tried, Esther! Every month I send requisitions to the hospital administrator. Every month I try to be as fair to colored as to white. And every month he tells me that the Board doesn't have the money."

She turned and eyed the young woman keenly. "That's neither here nor there. What I want you to understand is that you'll have to work under conditions as they are. Are you prepared for that?"

"No, ma'am," Esther said. "But I'll do my best. At least, the colored patients can have a good colored nurse."

Miss Head frowned. "Pretty confident, aren't you? Well, all to the good."

Esther said meekly, "I'll be here tomorrow, Miss Head," and turned to leave.

"Wait!" Miss Head said. "We've been honest so far. Let's go a little further."

Esther looked at her inquiringly.

"You know that the whole annex is run by colored nurses, such as they are, under the supervision of white supervisors?"

"Yes, ma'am. I know."

"Well, I may as well tell you what you probably know already. The supervisors hate it. I try to rotate them between these two buildings and the annex. But even if they have only one shift a week in the annex, they still hate it. These are the facts of life, Esther, and we can't escape them. I can't say I entirely lack sympathy for them. The working conditions are poor; and then—well, I have my own prejudices and can understand their attitude. Most decent white people are afraid to admit to prejudices, which only makes them worse, of course."

Esther nodded and kept her face expressionless.

"Now *you're* here," Miss Head continued, "and I don't see why, after two or three months, when you have the hang of things, you couldn't relieve one of the supervisors. In fact, if a few more Negro girls like you would go to a nurse's college, in time we might be able to head the whole annex with qualified colored supervisors." She sighed again. "Esther, you'll need more than your training here. You'll need a wisdom and self-control that I question you're capable of at your age."

"I'll do my best," Esther said simply. She surprised herself by what she said next. "Miss Head, I realize my responsibility here as the first qualified Negro nurse. And there's something I want to tell you now before I begin, so you'll never have reason to be disappointed in me."

"Yes?" The grey eyes assumed caution.

"I have a four-year-old illegitimate daughter." Her hands in her white gloves were cold.

There was a long silence in which the Director of Nurses merely looked thoughtful. She asked finally, "Would you say that you've been promiscuous since? Since the birth of your child, I mean?"

"No, I haven't."

"Then your personal life is nothing to me," Miss Head said calmly. "Do your work well, and you'll be made supervisor as I promised. As for this—I'm sure it's known in your community?"

Esther nodded.

"Nevertheless, you people seem to have a great capacity for tolerance. And after four years—well, I advise you merely to keep your mouth shut and your conduct discreet."

Esther had a longing to clasp hands with this woman who was bigger than her prejudices; to make with her the simple occidental gesture of mutual salute. But by custom it would not be done between them, and Esther gathered up her papers and departed after saying a somewhat stilted goodbye.

Chapter Twenty

IT DIDN'T come as a surprise to Esther when Lucy asked to be allowed to adopt Hope. Lucy had been hinting broadly at it for some time, and Sam had warned Esther of what was in his wife's mind.

"Lucy gets hold of an idea and worries it like a cat with a mouse," he said. "I can't do nothing with her. I'm telling you so's you'll be ready."

She was ready.

"Lucy, we've shared Hope since she was born. If she doesn't have a father, at least she's had two mothers. Don't ask this thing of me now. You know I can't give up my baby."

"I don't see why not. I've had her for four years, and she's more mine than yours. It's confusing for her to have to obey both you and me. Going back and forth like she is, that child ain't gonna have no security. All the psychology books say it's bad for a child not to have a stable home."

Esther couldn't help being amused. Lucy, who'd never been fond of books before, had now taken to reading everything she could find on the rearing of children.

"Of course it's bad, Lucy," Esther said. "But most of the world's children grow up in homes that aren't stable in the sense that the psychologists mean. Anyway, it's out of the question."

"You're just being selfish! You're not thinking of Hope's good. Why, me and Sam already feel like she's ours, and she needs both a father and a mother."

"That may be true, Lucy. But I am thinking of her. Hope's a lot like me, but she's a lot like her father too." Lucy looked at her sharply. Esther had never mentioned Paul before. She continued calmly. "And she'll need the one thing I can give her more than anything as she grows older."

"What's that?"

"Understanding," Esther said simply.

Lucy grew angry. "Seems to me, since she's so much like you, as you say, that's the one thing she don't need. If I remember, Grandear always claimed to understand you more'n she did me. You had plenty of understanding, all right; and look how you turned out!"

It was a direct slap, and Esther winced under it; but she answered with finality. "It won't do any good, Lucy. Hope's mine, and I intend to keep her, and do the best I can by her till she's grown. If you don't like the arrangement we have, I'll get Munsie to keep her while I'm at work."

"I didn't say I wouldn't keep her. You're not fair, Esther! You never was. You'll regret this, you'll see!"

Esther packed a small lunch that afternoon and took her child to the hill. It was a bright, cool September day, and they both wore sweaters. It was the first time that she'd taken Hope there.

"Where're we going, Mama?"

"To a secret place I know."

"What's there?"

"Lots of things, if you look for them."

An old lady stopped them on the way and exclaimed over Hope's beauty. She offered the little girl a nickel. Hope turned questioningly to Esther. "May I take it, Mama?"

Lucy would say no, Esther thought. "Yes, if you can give something for it."

"But I don't have anything to give!"

"Sure you do! A nice thank you, a smile, maybe a hug. Take your pick."

Hope considered. "I'll give you all of them," she said to the old lady, and suited her action to her words. The old lady went her way, beaming her momentary happiness.

Esther had a wry thought. Perhaps her sole criterion in making decisions concerning Hope was to do the opposite of what Lucy would have done. She was playing it by ear; but so far her ear seemed good.

The joy of the day and of being alone with her child took her suddenly. When they reached the clearing, she caught Hope up in her arms and ran with her to the top of the hill. Breathless and panting, she dropped the lunch box and threw herself down on the ground, Hope on top of her, laughing and nuzzling till they were both spent.

"Mama, I like Saturdays with you!" Hope exclaimed.

"Me too. Now, what d'you see?"

Hope looked around. "Nothing but trees and grass and some houses down there."

"Oh, then you're not looking where I am."

Hope regarded her mother, lying on her back on the grass, her eyes on the wide sky. She promptly followed suit.

"I see a cloud that looks like a cow," her mother said.

"Where?"

Esther pointed with a finger.

"Oh, I see it too. Mama, there's one like a dog! He's running!"

They played so for a while. Esther felt an enormous pride in her offspring's intelligence. Having peopled the sky with dogs and dragons and castles, they had their lunch and then began to discover the ground beneath them.

"See that ant with the big bread crumb?"

"Yes, Mama."

"That's a worker ant. He's taking the dinner home to the Mama ant and her babies. They live in that hole, along with lots of other ants. They call the Mama ant the queen."

"Is that the Papa ant?"

"No, Hope. He's just a worker ant."

"Well, where's the Papa ant?"

Esther felt that she'd undertaken more than she could cope with. "Papa ants don't live long, Hope."

"Why?"

"I don't know, darling."

Hope continued to watch the laborious process until the ant disappeared inside the hill. "Mama?"

"Yes, Hope?"

"Does everything have a Papa and a Mama?"

"Yes."

"And everybody too?"

"Yes, dear."

"Did you have a Papa?"

"Yes, I did," knowing what was coming next.

"Where is he?"

"He died and went to heaven."

"Mama, did my Papa die and go to heaven?" Her expression was casual. So she could be devious! Paul's child. Esther made a rapid decision. It was safest to tell the truth.

"No, dear. Your Papa is alive."

"Then how come I don't never see him?"

"Don't ever see him. Because your Papa and I don't live together, Hope."

"How come?"

"Because we didn't think we'd be happy together. When you're older you'll understand. I'll tell you all about it."

Hope nodded, thinking about it. After a moment she seemed satisfied. The five-o'clock freight began hoarsely to announce its arrival. "I don't like that noise, Mama," Hope said. "I get goose bumps."

"How strange!" Esther thought. She had never liked it, either. Hope was as much hers as Paul's. "I don't like it, either," Esther said aloud. "Let's sing so we won't hear it."

And they began to sing loudly: "Hickory, dickory, dock! The mouse ran up the clock . . ."

Chapter Twenty-one

THE MONDAY of her third week as nursing supervisor at Wharton Memorial Hospital, Esther walked to work. She walked the twenty-six blocks because she was early, and because the walk on that cool October day would do battle with the anger in her. The anger had grown more and more familiar during the past four months, stalking her, catching her unawares, inhabiting her. She was constantly on guard against it, knowing that it waited only for a weak moment to force her into the outburst that would destroy her.

It was what they were all waiting for—the Negro nurses, the white supervisors, Miss Head. . . .

"Well, how goes it? Think you're going to make it, Esther?" Miss Head knew full well how it went.

"It goes well," Esther lied emphatically.

Miss Head would nod then and raise her thick eyebrows to indicate she wasn't fooled. She was kindly, but she was practical. Esther had accepted the job knowing the circumstances, and as far as the Director was concerned, the girl could stick with it or leave it; but she couldn't help her.

Esther walked past the two tall brick buildings for whites through the gate that led to the colored annex. The brick here was dark as long-dried blood, not having been cleaned since the erection of the annex some twenty years before. Inside was little better—gloomy, dingy, slightly less than clean. When she arrived at the cubicle of an office that was hers during her eight-hour shift, she was still fifteen minutes early. The white supervisor on the midnight-to-eight shift, already dressed for the street, was putting on her coat.

"Good morning, Miss Noble," Esther said carefully and cheerfully.

"Nurse Kennedy," the woman acknowledged, giving her the briefest of glances. The white personnel, without exception, employed this form of address to avoid using the word Miss—to them a verbal symbol of equality. Miss Noble was not particularly antagonistic to Esther, although some of the supervisors were. But after a night in the annex none of them was inclined to be cordial.

Esther removed her coat. "How was Amanda Jones last night?"

Miss Noble shrugged. "Hollering and crying as usual. Her temperature's lower, though. The operation's scheduled for noon. You got two new accidents last night, if you can call them that. A man—somebody took a knife to him. The resident came over and sewed up his chest. And a woman—husband hit her over the head with a bottle. Concussion. She's still on critical. That Sampson girl's about ready for delivery. She's in the labor room."

"Then she's been prepared?"

"No," Miss Noble said coolly, looking at the clock, which meant that she was impatient to leave and that Esther would have to see that Stella Sampson was ready for delivery.

Esther picked up the phone and spoke to the nurse on the third floor. "Miss Taylor, please prepare Mrs. Sampson for delivery immediately, and contact her doctor. I'll be up shortly." She didn't look at Miss Noble, whose expression would show her faintly amused annoyance with the airs these colored nurses put on between themselves.

Esther went to work, not waiting for the clock. Whatever her shift, she could always count on having to complete the work of the supervisor who had preceded her—never too much, only enough to harass her. It was the gauntlet at her feet, daring her, nudging her to outburst. The white supervisors did not like working the annex; but they liked it less that a Negro could occupy the same position. And they waited in silent mocking anticipation for their small provocations to push her beyond her control.

But Esther's anger wasn't for them. All in all, they did what they had to do with the efficiency native to their training, and it wasn't Esther's nature to respond to petty goadings. There were larger things which deserved her anger, things that her mind still hadn't defined.

She took the single ancient elevator to the third floor. Miss Taylor, a squarely built woman with a dour expression, was the only nurse on obstetrics. She was a practical nurse who had worked in the annex all of its twenty years. Esther found her struggling with the rusty crank of Mrs. Sampson's bed, and grumbling.

"Don't know why the hell I don't quit this job. Nothing works around here. Trouble with the white folks' hand-me-downs is they ain't handed down soon enough. Everything's falling apart time we get it."

"Mrs. Sampson's ready?" Esther asked.

Miss Taylor looked up at her sourly. "Yeah, she's ready. I sent her on to delivery."

"Who's with her?"

"Who you expect? Nobody. The doctor'll be there right away, they say. But I expect he'll take his time, especially since she dragged him over here on a false alarm yesterday." She chuckled. "He was mad as hell. Tried to make her go back home, till he saw she was so scared it was better she stayed. Anyway, I got her ready, and that's all I can do for her. I got seventeen other patients in here to see to."

"Yes, but she really shouldn't be alone," Esther said with some firmness. "Her doctor expects breech birth, and this is her first."

Miss Taylor stopped her cranking and straightened up, a hand on her hip. "Now you look, Miss Kennedy. I've been in this hole about as long as you been living. I don't have no fancy degrees, but I know about all there is to know about nursing. I know her condition, but it's for her doctor to be seeing to her. It ain't that I don't feel for her; but I don't have no time to be holding her hand till that child decides to drop. I ain't got but two hands of my own. I got one woman had a Caesarean yesterday, and is still puking every minute, on the minute. The damn anesthetist musta gone wild. I got two starting on labor, and I got—"

Esther put a hand on her shoulder. She liked the old termagant, who reminded her faintly of Grandear. She said gently, "I know how it is. Let's just do the best we can, huh? I'll look in on Sampson."

"You do that," Miss Taylor retorted sharply. But she was mollified.

Mrs. Sampson was little more than a girl, and frightened. She was crying and wrestling with the straps Miss Taylor had fastened on her. When she saw Esther, she wailed aloud. "You-all fixing to leave me in here alone to die? Strap me down and leave me to die?"

"Oh no, we're not!" Esther said in a shushing voice. "Here now. The doctor'll be here in a minute."

The girl said pitifully, "I want my husband. They wouldn't let him come up to see me. I want my Billy."

"You'll see him right after the baby's born."

"Take the straps off. Please take them off," the girl pleaded hysterically.

"Of course." Esther complied, speaking softly all the while. She hated the idea of strapping down women in childbirth like animals; but this one had Dr. Whittaker, who believed in strapping, and from what Esther knew of him—cold, impersonal, brilliant—he would put the straps back on immediately he arrived.

He came shortly with two white nurses in tow. "Why

isn't she strapped?" he inquired impatiently of Esther. "Never mind. We'll take over now, Nurse."

"Don't leave me, Nurse!" the girl screamed. "Please!"

Esther gave her a reassuring smile. "I have to go. But it's all right. You'll be fine. Just do what your doctor says. You're going to be all right. Your baby too."

But they both knew she lied. Stella Sampson and her child would probably emerge from that room physically whole, because of Dr. Whittaker's skill. But the dread of childbirth and the place where she had been isolated in her pain and fright would linger, perhaps always.

Esther took the elevator back to the first floor. The expectant father in the waiting room was about nineteen. He had a sick, nervous look about him.

"The doctor's with your wife now, Mr. Sampson. You mustn't worry. Dr. Whittaker is a good doctor."

"Yes'm. You sure she'll be all right?" He twisted his hat uneasily in his hands. "I can't help worrying. Stella's so scared. And I'm scared mostly that she's mad at me."

"Why?"

"For giving her the baby," he said helplessly. "Looks like she's having such a hard time."

"Yes, she is," Esther said honestly. "But it'll be over soon. She's young and healthy. She'll come through all right. I know she isn't mad at you. She asked about you when I was there."

"She did? What she say?"

"Well . . ." She hesitated. "I guess she was missing you. How long've you been married?"

He grinned sheepishly. "Six months. I sure am glad she ain't mad."

"Not mad. Just scared." She touched his arm. "Billy, when you take her home, try to make it easy for her. You know how women are—they need a lot of petting and spoiling after having a baby. Bringing a child is hard work, you know."

He said earnestly, "I sure will, Nurse. I sure will."

Esther returned to the third floor to take a look at the infants in Ellen Dobbins' charge. She was pleased. Ellen was a twin, an intelligent bright-faced nurses' aid of eighteen. Her counterpart Helen, who worked in pediatrics across the hall, was as earnest and cheerfully industrious as she. They were, so far as Esther could see, the only two in the whole annex who took any joy in their work.

"I see the Capers baby has gained three ounces," Esther said, examining the chart.

"Oh, everybody was worried about that premie, but I knew he'd be all right."

Esther smiled at her. "Your tender loving care, Ellen?"

"Something like that." The girl grinned. And for the moment Esther was gladdened.

"I don't know what I'd do without you and Helen," she said, and was rewarded for saying it by the girl's gratified expression.

She walked down one flight to Surgical and went directly to the operating room. Amanda Jones's hysterectomy was scheduled for noon. The surgeon, Dr. Mason, would bring his own team of assistants, but everything must be ready and waiting when they arrived. She tested the lights, flipping the switches one after another. The lesser lights seemed in order, but the giant overhead cyclops flickered a little, dimmed, and then brightened again. Somewhere there was a defect in that light. She had noticed it before and had spoken to Miss Head about it. The Director had sent an electrician to see to it. The electrician had come, found the lights perversely working perfectly, remarked cheerfully that wiring installed twenty years ago had marvelous stamina, and departed. He had said that it was probably only a momentary failure at the plant.

Not convinced, Esther had spoken to Miss Head again. "Miss Head, even if there's nothing wrong with the wiring, suppose something happened at the plant during an operation. We don't even have an emergency generator in the annex. A patient could die!"

"Esther, don't be so dramatic!" Miss Head said sharply. "We have a generator over here. In fact, we have two. We could easily rush one over."

"Why can't we have one of them in the annex?" Esther persisted.

Miss Head's grey eyes met hers squarely. "Because the administrator won't allow it. There are ten times as many patients here as in the annex. We must think of them first. Esther, I warned you."

"Yes, ma'am, you did," Esther said, almost whispering it, so that her anger wouldn't erupt with the words.

Now again, she felt the rage and the helplessness. She turned abruptly and went to the female surgical ward. Amanda Jones, corpulent in her white gown, was screaming, "Oh, Lord Jesus! Oh, Lord Jesus!"

"Why don't you shut up?" Miss Holly said disgustedly, and jabbed a vicious needle into a huge buttock. The woman yelled again.

"Yeah! Shut up! Everybody in here's sick!" another woman said.

Miss Holly saw Esther and swabbed diligently.

"What're you giving her?" Esther asked.

"Penicillin. Six hundred thousand units, like Dr. Mason ordered." Miss Holly was a fairly young woman, better trained than most of the nurses, having had a two-year course at a normal school. But she was careless in her duties, and sometimes sadistic in her treatment of the patients.

Esther pulled the screen around the bed. "He didn't order you to try to break the needle in her," she said tersely. "And the rule is that screens are always to be drawn when a patient's body must be exposed."

Miss Holly regarded her with some disdain. She spoke loudly for the benefit of the listening patients in the ward. "You don't like the way I give hypos, you just come give them yourself, Sugar. This old whore deserves no better."

"She's mean, that's what that bitch is!" Amanda complained snifflingly to Esther. "Here I am about to lose my womanhood, and she got no sympathy, no feelings. Treat folks like dogs! Shaved me right in front of everybody and wouldn't even pull the screen. You heard what she called me? Whyn't you fire her now you's a supervisor, Miss Kennedy?"

Ada Holly gave a sniff of amusement. "Yes. Why don't you just do that little thing, Miss Kennedy?"

Esther could feel the women beyond the screen straining to hear. She said distinctly, "Miss Holly, I have no authority to fire you, as you well know. But I do have the authority to report you to the Director, and I won't hesitate to do so if this happens again. Speaking to a patient like that is unforgivable."

Miss Holly's eyes stared into hers boldly for a moment; then grew fearful and dropped away before reassuming their insolence. Esther had won that round. Ada Holly had no respect for her nor for her professional tone; what she feared was the white authority, the white reproof.

"There's a few things I could tell Miss Head about you too, you know."

"There's nothing you can tell Miss Head about me that she doesn't already know," Esther said coldly. "Now you have one hour to finish up in here. At exactly ten, I'll send Miss Crawford to cover for you and I'll expect you in my office for a conference. Be there, Miss Holly!"

Esther was surprised at the total authority in her voice. She left the ward, walking quickly, but not so quickly that she didn't hear the loud appreciative remarks of the women.

"That one got your water on, ain't she, Holly?" . . . "Yes, Lord. I'd say the witch on this ward better straighten up on her broomstick and fly right, wouldn't you?"

In the hall, Esther leaned against the wall and breathed deeply. She had won that round, but Ada Holly came in many sizes and shapes in the colored annex at Wharton Memorial. Now that Esther had struck her first blow the news would spread, and her adversary would grow stronger. The thing was that she still didn't know what she fought. It was the boxing at shadows that was wearing her down.

"I been lying here in this bed," the old man in Male Medical said. "And I been looking out that window night and day. You know, Miss, when you's old like me and 'bout to die, ain't nothing to do but look and think, when the pain lets you."

Esther took his hand. "Come now, Mr. Trimble. You're not *about* to die." But she knew that he was. He was old, and it was too late to stop the malignancy that was eating at his vitals.

"Don't matter none now," he said, turning gentle eyes on her. "Sooner it happens, happier I'll be. I done made my peace with the Lord. But lying here, I been thinking how it is in this place. I look out over there where it's all clean and bright, and I watch the white folks come and go. I know there's misery over there like it is here. But the nurses and doctors all seems so busy and brisk. It's different with us colored folks. Seems like everybody comes in here real slow, sort of tired-like. Nurses and attendants all sad and sour, excepting you and the two little nurses what works with the children. And I gets to wondering how that is."

"It's because we don't have enough nurses. They're all overworked." She spoke impersonally, because if she let him the old man would talk on and on. But he held to her hand.

"No'm. It ain't that. That's only part of it. Like the way things look around here—that's only part of it. Even if everything was all new and bright and we had all the nurses and things we need, it wouldn't make it right all the way."

Suddenly, Esther was listening intently. "What would?" she asked.

He was silent for a while, turning his head and looking out the window. Then he said irrelevantly, "I been sick a long time. Before I came to the hospital, the pain in my body wasn't no less than it is now. Fact is, 'twas worse without the medicines. And I didn't have nobody to give me the care I gets here. But seems like since I been in this place I done got a pain in my heart."

"You mean you're homesick?"

He smiled. "For my little piece of land and my shack? I reckon so, Miss. But you ain't understanding me. I ain't homesick so much for myself. I mean I'm feeling the lone-someness of all folks, white and black—then what is treated like us, and even them that ain't. You ever have a dog, Miss?"

"No, I never did."

"Well, I had one. I was a young man then, with no family. And I had this dog. Just a little old mongrel he was. But he was all I had. I took him with me everywhere, and we'd eat together. Sometimes when 'twas cold we'd sleep together."

Esther sighed. He would ramble on now. She should break away, but she hadn't the heart. It seemed so important to the old man to say what he had to say.

"I got myself a wife after a while. She was a good woman, but she didn't like no dogs in the house. So to please her, I built my dog a house for himself and made him stay out there nights. It was a good house, warm, dry, had a mat on the floor. But I guess before that, Champ never thought 'bout him being a dog. All he knew was he was in the family where he belonged. But when I put him out, he knew it all right. Howled every night, and wouldn't eat for a long time. Then after he got the idea, he started acting like a dog. Turned mean and snappish as could be. Bit a plug out of me one day. I didn't want to do it, but my old lady finally called the dog-catcher to come for him. You see, Miss," Mr. Trimble said sadly, "his mind and his heart was sick, 'cause we'd cut him out from his rightful place, and after that he didn't know how to act, but like a dog."

Esther nodded, understanding at last what the dying man was saying, seeing the enemy for the first time clearly; the giant, implacable enemy against which her own puny anger was futilely pitted.

"Miss, it's the being cut off—the way it makes us feel like we's dogs, even though we're part of the human race. It's that more'n anything that makes it the way it is. And when we find ain't nothing we can do about it, we gives up and turns around and acts like dogs 'cause we is treated like dogs. These nurses round here that walk so slow with the food and medicine, they is given up because they know, no matter what they do for the sick bodies, they can't cure the sickness in the souls. Of course, we is more or less cut off everywhere. But when you feeling poorly, and can look out the windows and see the difference so clear, it probably hurts the most."

"You must get some sleep now, Mr. Trimble."

"Yes'm, I will," he promised obediently. But he wasn't through. He continued earnestly: "Miss, I said these things to you because that's how I was thinking till you came. Then I got to thinking some more. I seen you ain't got the sickness yet. And because you got a place here ain't no colored folks had before, I wants you to know it gives me encouragement. I speaks to you so because I want you to keep on keeping on. We ain't no dogs, and we don't ought to give up just because it's hard. If we knows we's in the human family, we got to find our way in and sit down at the table if it takes all the strength and years we got. Ain't that right, Miss? Ain't that right?"

He was gripping her arm. "That's right, sir. But you must sleep now." She made him more comfortable and gave him a cool drink, for he was wrought up from his talk.

He said before she left him, "You know, Miss, sometimes I wonder if deep in their hearts, white folks ain't as lonesome with us outside as I was for my dog. Sometimes I think they is. After all, they's human too."

She left him and finished her inspection of Medical, and then went back to her office to await Miss Holly. She sat quietly, for her anger had left her. In its place was a calm clear resolution, put there by the words of an old man whose dying thoughts were for the "lonesomeness of all folks, white and black."

Chapter Twenty-two

THE FOLLOWING Saturday, Esther went downtown in search of battery lamps. It took her some time to find the kind she wanted, and they cost more than she'd expected. She ordered six of the lamps to be sent to the annex, and then hurried to the bank. She had to get there before it closed, because she didn't even have carfare left.

She got to the bank ten minutes before it closed. She had to wait another five minutes for her turn at the cashier's window. While the woman was checking Esther's account, a man came up and spoke to her. Esther was impatient, for she had other things to do downtown that Saturday. Then the man turned away from the window and his eyes met Esther's. For a moment she felt dizzy and gripped the edge of the counter; but she couldn't look away. It was Paul Miller.

He had recognized her, for he stood still, staring at her. Then he strode rapidly away to an office beyond and closed the door behind him. The enamel plate on the door read: Mr. P. Miller, Loan Officer.

"How you want this, singles or fives? What's the matter, girl? You sick or something?" The cashier's face was solicitous.

"No. No, I'm all right, thanks."

Esther took the money and fled, almost knocking down the guard who stood at the door. "Sorry," she said, and was grateful for the belligerent look he gave her. It cleared her head.

"Esther, what's troubling you?" Munsie asked. "You ain't heard a word I said this evening. You sick or something?"

"No, just tired, I guess."

Munsie was a regular visitor these days. She would come over in the evenings, bringing her boy Ishmael, who was now seven years old. Ish would play patiently with Hope while their mothers talked. Munsie came because she was lonely; and Esther, who understood loneliness, welcomed her.

"I guess I did kinda miss that part. What were we talking about, Munsie? Pa's birthday?"

"I was doing the talking, Sugar, like always. And that's okay as long as you're doing the listening. We been through with Pa's birthday long time. You don't need to worry about that no more. Just give me the money and I'll tend to everything. We was on something else."

Munsie had a merry streak in her and her chatter was usually full of gaily implausible anecdotes. But tonight she had chosen a theme. "I was talking 'bout these no-good men we got here in South Leemouth. They come around all wanting the same thing. Not that I'm all that righteous, but I can't be bothered. They got no money, no manners, and no morals. All they got is . . ." She made an obscene gesture and laughed uproariously. Munsie talked with all her rotund little body and her comic button face.

"I tell them if they can sit me down so I won't have to take in white folks' washing, and take care of me and Ish so we won't have to want for nothing, then I'll consider it. I'm thirty years old, and all a piece of trim can do for me now is give me three troubles instead of two. Last one I told that to was so scared he took off and left his hat in my parlor." She laughed again. "Lord, I sure am glad you got rid of them roomers, Esther. Sure couldn't let myself go when them Church of God folks was around!" She howled again. But when her laughter subsided, she took on a wistful expression.

"But 'tain't so funny. Sometimes I'm mighty lonesome for a man. Ain't you, Esther?"

Esther thought that her lonesomeness was for Joe, for Joe, for Joe. . . . But she couldn't bring herself to say that. She made a rueful grimace which Munsie took for an answer.

"Seems to me life ain't fair! All the good men are married, and most of them to women who don't appreciate them. Look at Lucy, for instance. Sam Adams is a wonderful husband to her. He works hard and gives her everything she wants. He don't drink or gamble or run around. But does she appreciate it? She does not! All she does is nag and nag. 'Go back and wipe your shoes, Sam! I just waxed the floor. Hang up your coat, Sam!' You ever watch them together? He try to put his arm around her or kiss her, and she shoves him off like he wasn't clean or something. 'Sam, you'll muss my hair! You stop that foolishness!' "

Munsie's mimicry of Lucy was perfect, and Esther couldn't help laughing.

"Bet that man don't get no nooky from that one more'n once a month, if that often," Munsie said darkly. "I'll tell you something, Esther. A man like that deserves better than an old maid like Lucy."

"Yes, he does," Esther agreed sadly. It was true. Lucy took Sam so much for granted now that she made few efforts to please him. Often Esther caught an expression of hurt bewilderment in his eyes at Lucy's outbursts; and she grieved for him, for she loved him dearly. But there was nothing she could do for them. Lucy seemed incapable of loving anyone except Hope. The fact was, that the less she seemed to love others, the more she appeared to love the child.

Hope, a gay and self-reliant little girl, shook off Lucy's smothering with the instinct of the inviolable innocent. She would clamber over Sam, hugging and kissing him on demand. She had ecstasies of "I love you, Mama!" And she was as freely abandoned with Pa and Munsie. But her response to Lucy's affection was friendly, matter-of-fact, muted.

This, oddly, only seemed to increase Lucy's devotion. She grudged the time the child spent with her mother. Every evening when Esther came from work, Lucy would say, "Seems like she could stay home with me *one* night!" Esther had given up reminding her that Hope's home was with her. When she worked the night shift, Lucy complained about Hope's days "away from home."

Often Esther's mind pondered the imponderable that was

Lucy. But tonight, after Munsie left with Ish and Hope was put to bed, she sat for a while at the dining-room table. She was thinking of Paul.

Her shock at seeing him had subsided. It was natural enough that she should see him sometime in a town the size of Leemouth. She analyzed her reactions. It was not hate she felt. Not fear. Not even revulsion. She was not sure what it was. But he had fathered her child, and seeing him again had triggered a violent emotion in her.

What was it, she wondered, that she had seen in *him* as he stood there staring at her? He was not, somehow, the same Paul she had once known. He seemed quieter now, more sensible, the sober businessman working at his uncle's bank. And in his face she had seen—shame? embarrassment? guilt? None of these. She had seen in him only what she had felt in herself: the acknowledgment of the bond between them, an almost mystical remnant of their mutually degrading experience.

She had, as she sat there, a wildly sacrilegious thought. That God Himself was blind to the nature of human experiences; and that He used them only for a single, patient, implacable purpose: to attach the human heart, as with so many inseverable strings of its own making, one to the other, one to the other, and finally perhaps to Himself.

Chapter Twenty-three

"CAN'T YOU even get us enough paint to do the beds?" Esther asked.

Miss Head was tapping out an impatient tattoo on her desk. Her grey eyes were angry. "Esther, you're turning this into a pitched battle between us, and I don't like it! You just won't understand that I do and have done all I can."

"But surely a few gallons of paint! The attendants will do the work in their spare time."

"Spare time?" The bushy eyebrows went up. "Well, that would be for you to settle with them. What you've got to understand is that I've gone the limit. You've been a supervisor just seven weeks, and you've been a monkey on my back ever since you began. I've done all I can to help you. I let you goad the attendants into washing down the walls. I kept you three weeks on the day shift so you could supervise that. I even managed to have the heating system overhauled. And I got you the new kitchen utensils, didn't I?"

"Yes, but a little paint would—"

"Even one gallon of paint is out of the question," Miss Head said shortly. "I've vexed the administrator too much already. He made it clear to me, and I will make it clear to you. The colored section of this hospital will get what is absolutely necessary and no more!"

Esther was silent.

"Well, what do you want me to do?" Miss Head exclaimed in exasperation. "Go over his head to the Board of Directors? You're the most bull-headed Negro girl I've met!"

After a moment, Esther said thoughtfully, "No, you couldn't do that; but could you give me a list of the people on the Board?"

The Director leaned back in her chair to stare at her. "Why?"

"I'd just like to know, that's all."

"Why do you want it?"

Esther met her eyes with her own troubled gaze. "I don't quite know myself. I just have a feeling I ought to know who's on the Board."

Miss Head raised her eyes to the ceiling, a despairing gesture. "You people and your feelings! Well, I have a feeling I ought not to do this, but I guess if you tried hard enough you could find out for yourself. And you would." She handed Esther a sheet of stationery. "Here, you'll find all the members listed on the letterhead."

Esther studied the list for a long time. Then she spoke carefully. "This Mr. Miller who's Chairman of the Board —he's the one that owns the syrup business?"

Miss Head made a wry moue. "The same. Currently our richest citizen, and therefore our most influential. He's chairman of everything nowadays. In this instance, I don't think he does more than lead the letterhead."

Esther nodded, still examining the list. "And Mr. Brookhouser—the bank president?"

"Yes. Every one rich, powerful, and unconcerned with the colored annex. Now are you satisfied?"

"Yes'm. And thank you," Esther said meekly.

She went back to the annex feeling strangely excited. She wasn't sure why. The feeling of excitement lingered even after it was reported to her that in her absence Mr. Trimble had lapsed into a coma and as quickly died. The nurse who reported it was surprised to hear Esther exclaim, "Thank God!" and took it as being something of a desecration. The dead were accorded a good deal more respect than the living in the annex. But Esther could feel only joy that the old man's sufferings of both body and mind were ended.

Early that afternoon, a new patient arrived in Surgical— the Reverend Sylvester Billingsley. Esther, having just worked the four-to-midnight shift for two weeks, was again back on eight-to-four duty.

"You'd better come see about him," Miss Sanders, the nurse in Male Surgical, said. She was a tight little knot of a woman. "He been hollering and calling for you since he got here. I got a suspicion the old goat thinks he's fixing to enter the pearly gates and ain't too happy about it. I'm a Methodist myself."

"What's his trouble?"

"Appendectomy. Eight in the morning. Doctor Morgan. There's ten church sisters in the waiting room moaning and praying."

"What's he want me for?"

"God knows. Pulling strings, I guess. Says he's known you all your life. Guess he thinks you can make sure he keeps on living."

"We got any arsenic around here?" Esther asked innocently.

The nurse stared, fumbled with the idea, and then laughed hilariously, slapping her skinny thighs. She poked a friendly finger at Esther. "Girl! I didn't used to think much of you. But you're all right! More I see of you, more I say it: You're all right! Arsenic! Hooee!" And she went off, still laughing.

Esther considered whether or not she should go to the minister. She didn't have to, and she certainly didn't want to. Since Grandear's funeral she had hated the sight of him. She never attended his church, she refused to have him visit her, and she avoided him whenever he was at Pa's. Sick or well, she wanted nothing to do with him. But she remembered that Grandear had been a regular communicant at his church, even though she had often called him "a hypocritical bag of chicken-shit."

When she could bring herself to it, Esther went to his bedside.

The Rev. Billingsley was in one of the annex' six inelegant private rooms, a mountain of uneasy flesh beneath the white sheet. Esther found him clutching a Bible and praying audibly, with beads of sweat glistening on his forehead. He opened his eyes when she entered, and made a ludicrous attempt at a smile.

"I'm glad you've come, Esther."

"How're you feeling, Reverend?"

"Poorly, child. Poorly."

"You'll feel better after the operation."

His eyes betrayed a genuine fright at the word, and a hint of tears. He reached a pudgy hand out for hers. "Child, I feel my time has come," he said sententiously.

Esther stifled a giggle. "Nonsense, Reverend! It'll take more than a simple appendectomy to get rid of you. And you have a good surgeon. There's nothing to worry about."

He shook his head. "Esther, ain't nothing the doctors can do when the Lord sends the black angel. And I had a dream last week."

"You ate too much before going to bed," Esther said coldly. "That wasn't the Lord's fault."

Before her eyes he began to melt, to quiver, to slobber as he talked. "Esther, the more I pray, the scareder I get. I always was afraid of operations. I used to think I had faith in the Lord's will for me. But I don't want to die! Help me, child! I don't want to die!"

"Then don't!" Esther said. She had come prepared to cheer and console, although she didn't like the man. But seeing him now reduced to a bloated caricature of a blubbering child made her ashamed for him. It was not his fright that annoyed her. She had seen enough of its presence to know that death was an enemy that people naturally feared. It was not even that the minister's fears were unwarranted. It was his refusal to give fight—his sniveling acceptance of his fear that outraged her sense of decency. She spoke in her anger.

"You're not going to die, I tell you. But if you think you are, nothing I can say will change your mind. And if you're so set on it, you just might, at that. But I can tell you one thing. I've seen many a person knew he was fixing to die —young and old—all kinds—and I've seen some that were afraid and some that weren't. But everyone I've seen was either ready to go, or fought like hell. I've always thought it was a sort of pride in human beings, something inside them that naturally makes them fight back at anything that's forced on them against their will, even death itself. But you aren't ready, and you aren't fighting. And Reverend, to tell you the truth, I don't know what you want me to do for you. I'll see that you get good attention, if that's what you want."

He stopped weeping to stare at her. "You got no pity!"

"No. Because you've got no pride!"

He took pride into himself then like a visible and instantaneous transfusion. "I got pride. You're wrong, Esther. I got pride. If I been lying here feeling scared, it's because the flesh is weak. But I'll show you I got pride. And I ain't called you in here to ask you no special favors like you think. I called you because I want to make you a confession and ask your forgiveness."

He was perspiring again. Esther took a towel and began to wipe his forehead. "A confession?"

"Yes. It's two things I got to confess to you. Don't care what you say, when a man goes under that knife, ain't no law says he got to come out. And I want to go with my soul clean."

Esther felt the first stirrings of pity for him. She said gently, "Not me, Reverend. You just talk to God about it."

He caught her hand again. "No. I got to say this. The first thing is about your Grandear's funeral—the things I said. I didn't mean no harm to you. I was just grieved to see the pain you'd laid on that good woman's heart. Then I found out the circumstances later. But that don't excuse me, 'cause the Bible say don't judge. And I confess to you that I is judged you, and judged you wrong, Esther. And I put wrong ideas in people's heads."

Esther sighed. "It's over now, Reverend. I don't hold it against you."

"The second thing," he continued determinedly, "is about the money."

"What money?" She was puzzled.

"The money your Grandear left you. I always did think you was a wild, reckless girl, and after everything happened like it did, the devil got to talking to me, telling me you didn't deserve that money, and showing me all it could do for Ebenezer Baptist Church. I sent the church sisters over with all kind of fine arguments to get you to give up the money to the church."

Esther smiled at that. "I did notice a lot of them hanging around about that time."

"Oh, that ain't all! After they couldn't get nothing from you, I got mad and did a bad thing—a real bad thing. Esther, you know that old shiftless Nackey Bates—in and out of jail all the time?"

Esther nodded, full of a sudden mirth.

"Well, he was claiming to have got religion long about that time. And I kinda put it in his mind that he'd be doing the Lord a good turn if he could transfer that money from you to Ebenezer, with a little left over for his services, of course."

Esther laughed, peal after peal of laughter, till tears ran down her cheeks. The Reverend, watching, smiled waveringly and then began to chuckle. "Yeah, it sure seems funny now I think about it. But that time I wasn't doing it for no joke." His face sobered. "The devil sure had me fast, Esther, and deceived me into thinking I was the Lord's agent. I even got to talking so smooth to Nackey, he thought it was his own idea. Anyway, he never found the money."

"He did try, you know."

"Yes. And it's been on my conscience ever since. Esther, before I goes into that operating room, I wants to hear you say you forgive this erring servant of God."

She patted his hand. "I forgive you, Reverend. Now try to rest."

He drew her hand to his lips and kissed the back of it, a slobbery smack. "I shoulda always known that anybody Lydia Jones loved much as she loved you had to be full of the spirit of the Lord."

Esther escaped as fast as possible.

She left the hospital premises as soon as the white supervisor arrived, and hurried home to help Munsie prepare for Pa's birthday party. But preoccupied as she was, the edges of her mirth still lingered, and she felt a small joy that she no longer hated the Reverend Sylvester Billingsley.

Chapter Twenty-four

IN THE center of the table there were two great iced cakes, each bearing forty candles. It was typical of Munsie that she had baked an extra cake when she discovered that one wouldn't hold eighty candles.

"That extra one is for you to take home to nibble on, Pa," Munsie said.

"I'll send a big piece to Joe," he answered. "I do wish he coulda been here."

The old man, dressed in his best suit and ensconsed at the head of the table, beamed on them all. "This here's been like one of Lydia's feasts," he said, his false teeth clicking. "Seems like I can feel her here in this room blessing us all."

"Don't talk like that now, Pa!" Lucy said sharply.

He turned mild eyes on her. "Don't fret now, Lucy. It's natural enough I should mention your Grandear. When you get my age, you'll know it's all the same with those we love. The living and the dead ain't all that far apart. Yessir! I feel them all the time—my wife, and my daughter, and my own parents. If your Grandear's here smiling on us all, ain't no reason for you to be upset, is there?"

"Sure not!" Munsie said before Lucy could answer. "You ready for the lighting of the candles now, Esther?"

"Whoa now!" Sam said, his big frame shaking the table a bit as he rose. "We got to let this dinner settle first. Ish and Hope is got some entertainment planned, ain't you, kids?"

Hope and Ishmael giggled simultaneously as they joined Sam at the foot of the table.

"All right, Ish," Sam prompted.

Ish made a flourish of a bow. "To Pa and friends," he said in his confident boy's voice. "Hope and me are happy to entertain you-all on this most special occasion of Pa's eightieth birthday."

The children went through a simple routine of action songs and recitations.

"They been practicing two weeks," Sam whispered to Esther. "I thought this piece was too hard for Hope, but she learned it wonderful!"

"Sam, *you're* wonderful!" Esther breathed, a little teary at seeing Hope, a blue fairy in her organdie dress, solemnly reciting her piece.

"I got all the pieces out of a book I been keeping since I was a boy," Sam said proudly.

Lucy shushed at them. Esther noted sadly that her sister's eyes were rapt, adoring the child. She turned her mind away from that to the happier fact that Hope was a born ham, gesturing and posing as she recited. At one point she forgot the words, and Ishmael supplied them in a stage whisper. Hope nodded a solemn thanks to him and completed the verse without further mishap. Then she made elaborate curtseys to Pa and the guests. Everyone clapped for her. Ish clapped harder than anyone. "You're good, Hope," he said.

Hope squirmed out of Lucy's overpowering embrace and ran to him, clapping herself and jumping gleefully. "Clap some more, Ish," she said. And they all laughed at that.

Pa said appreciatively, "Lord, Esther, that's a smart young-'un you got there. But Munsie, your Ish is the smartest. He knowed both their pieces."

"He learned them so's he could help her out if she needed it," Sam said. "Was more anxious for her to do right than himself."

"I kinda think he got a crush on Hope," Munsie laughed.

Hope snickered at that, while Ish merely looked as if he hadn't heard. But Lucy turned on Munsie with some venom. "Don't you say that!"

"Oh, God, what the hell's the matter with you now?" Munsie snapped back.

Lucy subsided, as was her way when counterattacked. "You just ought not to say things like that in front of them, that's all."

"Well, I guess it's time for the cake now, ain't it, Esther?" Sam said heartily.

"Yes. Munsie, light the candles now, will you?"

"Sure thing!"

Munsie had trouble getting the first candle lit. The match went out.

"Here, let me help you," Sam said.

Munsie handed him the box of matches. He lit one for himself and one for her. In the brief flare of the matchlight Esther caught the expression on both their faces. His was merely kind, open, friendly. But on Munsie's face there was the unmistakable look of a woman in love. And Esther pitied her—pitied her.

Chapter Twenty-five

IT STARTED storming during the night. Esther realized, as a violent peal of thunder shocked her out of sleep, that it was no ordinary storm. She got up and went to the next room to look at her child. Hope was sleeping peacefully in the bed that once had been Esther's. Her hair was a tangle of curls. Her long lashes lay flat on her cheeks like a doll's. She had half kicked the covers off, and one leg was entangled intricately in the blanket. Her bare toes seemed to her mother utterly defenseless.

Gently, Esther rearranged the covers. Hope stirred, smiled, threw one arm over her head, but didn't wake. Esther stood over her for a long time while the wind shook the old house. At intervals flashes of lightning would illuminate the child, the bed, the little slippers on the floor. For a short while hail fell in small pebbles on the roof. It was a tornado, then!

Esther smiled to herself. Like Hope, she had slept through many of them; had often slept the sounder because of them. Awake now, only because of the instinct to assure her young's safety, she was fully at peace, for the while detached from all concern about the future, her own or Hope's. For it seemed to Esther then less important that her child was female and fatherless than that she could sleep through a storm.

The storm abated about six, but rain still fell drearily and the sun didn't show. Leemouth went to work in wet and near-total darkness.

At eight twenty-five that morning, a sizzling noise was

heard in the light directly over the operating table, and simultaneously every light in Wharton Memorial Colored Annex went out.

When it happened, Dr. Morgan, who had just made a neat, skilled incision in the patient's abdomen, was in the act of receiving the first clamp from the instrument nurse. "The emergency generator—quick!" He spoke in a terse, unpanicked tone.

For the space of two breaths no one moved. Then in the semi-darkness the anesthetist spoke. "There isn't one over here, sir. We have to send over to Main for it."

"In the meantime, a flashlight, a lamp, anything! I've *got* to clamp!" Dr. Morgan's voice was more strained now.

The nurse nearest the door said, "I'll see to it," and flew to the telephone in the hall.

"Sponge," Dr. Morgan said to the nurse at his side. "Another. That's right, keep feeding them. Another minute without light and we're gonna lose this overfed nigger preacher," he muttered grimly.

"You're damn right," the anesthetist said with feeling.

At that moment, three Negro nurses entered the room, each carrying two oversized battery lamps.

"We're not sterile, doctor," Esther said, "but we'll stand away from you."

"Sterile, hell!" Dr. Morgan said. "Just hold those lamps closer, dammit!"

Once, as the operation proceeded, Ellen Dobbins swayed a little and Esther said sharply, "Don't you dare, Ellen."

Five minutes later, the generator arrived, hauled by two panting attendants, and the Negro nurses with their lamps were dismissed. Dr. Morgan, busily bent over the still form of the Reverend Billingsley, paid no attention.

"He going to live?" Helen asked Esther out in the hall.

"Sure. He'll live."

"I wasn't fixing to faint, Miss Kennedy," Ellen said reproachfully. "I was just excited. I never saw an operation before."

"Me neither," Helen acknowledged. "Gee, weren't we dramatic, though! Walking in there and saving old Billingsley's life, while those dumb white folks were still trying to haul that generator over here!"

"We were dramatic all right," Esther said, smiling at their two like faces.

"Right out of the movies we were!" Ellen agreed emphatically. "Although in the movies we'd have been white, of course."

The twins giggled simultaneously. Helen stopped giggling first. "Say! Where'd those lamps come from, anyway? They weren't around here before."

"We've had them a while," Esther said easily.

"Uh-hmm. I'll bet I know how they got here in the first place." Ellen's brown eyes were admiring, and a trifle wistful. "Miss Kennedy, you think Helen and me will ever get a chance to be real qualified nurses like you? Seems like we can't save enough out of what we make to get us started. If we could just get started!"

"You'll get started," Esther said. "Now get a move on with those lamps. Two to a floor. It's the best we can do for now."

"Little did I know," the Reverend Billingsley said with great sentimentality, "when I spoke to you that night before the operation that you would be the one to save my life. I can't thank you enough, Esther. I don't know how to thank you."

"Oh, I know a way," Esther said lightly.

He was taken aback, even in his weakness. But he said stoutly, "I'll do anything you ask."

Esther grinned wickedly at him. "When you're stronger, I'll hold you to that, Reverend."

She was delighted with her planned blackmail. Ebenezer Church, so efficient at raising money at their pastor's request, would soon be undertaking a new project—the raising of the scholarship funds necessary to put the Dobbins twins through a college for nurses.

Chapter Twenty-six

ESTHER HAD no trouble getting in to see Paul. She merely said that she wished to speak to Mr. Miller, the Loan Officer, and after waiting a while, the girl out front let her in and shut the door. He showed no astonishment at seeing her, only some suspicion and some relief. She guessed he had expected to see her again.

It would have been unthinkable for him to stand; but he indicated a chair. "Sit down, Esther."

For a long strained moment they looked at each other. Esther had despised the pride that had made her dress so carefully that morning; but now she was glad of it. "I came to ask a favor of you, Mr. Miller."

His expression said that he had known as much. Some of

the old sardonic Paul touched his blue eyes, widening them into a stare. Esther met his gaze calmly. She was not as nervous as she had expected to be. She said, "I think you do owe me a favor."

He was on sure ground now, fully the Paul she'd known. "I think you're wrong, Esther. I could hardly owe you anything."

She said slowly, "Then perhaps you owe a debt to your conscience."

He shook his head wonderingly at her. "Won't I ever be free of you? I was nothing but a boy—and you were only a colored servant!"

"But what you did has haunted you?"

He stared at her without answering.

"I was able to come because I thought so," Esther said quietly. She smiled then, lifting her chin slightly. "You see, I don't come for myself. I never would for myself. I—"

He interrupted her. "What do you want? Money?"

"No. I want you to use your influence to have a new and decent colored annex built at Wharton Memorial Hospital."

"What!" His face was a study in incredulity.

She went on relentlessly. "Your father's Chairman of the Board, and your uncle's a member. Together they have enough power to do it, and from what I remember you can get your folks to do just about anything for you."

"Well, I'll be!" He was still staring. "Girl, I used to think I was imagining what you were like. But you're even more so! You know what you're asking?"

"Yes. I've thought about it for some time."

"Well, why? What's your interest in this hospital?"

She told him at length—about her position there, about the dreary conditions, about the air of defeat and apathy among the staff. She waxed declamatory as she went on. "It's a place where the sick have no incentive to get well. Besides, it's not half big enough!" Then, realizing that his eyes were amused, she sighed. "I didn't mean to take the pulpit, but you can see how close this is to me."

"And for this you're blackmailing me, little black Esther?" His voice was soft and his eyes mocked. But somewhere within them, Esther saw a fleeting likeness to Hope's.

"Yes and no," she said grimly. "No, because I couldn't anyway. I knew that before I came. And yes, because when I saw you the other day, I felt maybe you had after all some spark of human decency, something in you that would make you happy to atone for what you did to me."

He asked broodingly, irrelevantly, "You went to college?"

"Yes."

"I thought so. You speak well. But you did then." He smiled. "I think that's one reason I found you extraordinary."

Esther lifted her eyebrows. "Why? Because I didn't say dis and dat like something out of a white man's pipe dream?"

"No. Because you've somehow escaped our national phobia; fear of seeming pompous. We'd rather be considered vulgar than correct. Tell me, Esther: your Grandmother— the one with the touch of greatness—is she well?"

Tears sprang to her eyes suddenly. She forced them back. "She died."

"I see." He nodded thoughtfully and then frowned, a dark, angry look, the one he'd been stalling to avoid. "Human decency, huh?"

Esther aimed deliberately. "Perhaps you can atone for what you did to yourself."

"How the hell do you know what I did to myself?"

"I know," she answered simply.

He leaned back in his chair, thoughtful again. "You probably do. Do you know that that cross was also my salvation, Esther? For the first time I saw myself clearly. . . ."

She said quickly and firmly, "I don't want to know about that. I think what happened, happened mostly because we were trying to know too much about each other. It can't be done here. At least not yet."

"Not ever!" he said to her, and it was a flat declaration to both of them of his final acknowledged allegiance. In his own mind, Paul had at last accepted his role as a southerner and a gentleman. But what he said next surprised her. "Had we lived somewhere else, under different circumstances, it wouldn't have happened. But we might have been friends."

It was futile to answer that. She said, "Anyway, will you do what you can for the annex?"

"Will its problems be solved then?" he countered.

She looked at him tiredly. "No, of course not. Its main problem is that it is an annex. But what can be done now should be done."

After a moment he said, "I can't promise you anything, except that I'll try."

"I believe you. For that I can promise you something. I'll never come again." She got up and turned to leave.

"I take it," he drawled lazily, "that nothing happened as a result of that unfortunate afternoon?"

She turned back to look at him; and had the momentary illusion that it was Hope's face looking at her with the anxious, wistful expression that meant she'd been naughty.

She would do it quickly now, cut Hope forever free from the possibility of her father's protection and patronage. Hope's might be a rocky journey, and she might someday curse her mother for what she did now. But she would never be the tortured mulatto in times of distress found, because it was easiest to justify it then, fawning at her father's back door.

And she would cut him free too. He would need to mail no discreet checks to assuage his own enduring guilt. Nor would he have to live with the secret recurring yearning to know the child he had fathered.

She said in simple kindness, "No, nothing happened, Paul."

PART THREE ⇛⇛⇛⇛⇛⇛⇛⇛⇛⇛⇛⇛⇛⇛⇛⇛⇛⇛⇛↘

Chapter Twenty-seven

THREE YEARS later Joe Mead returned to South Leemouth to set up his practice. He was a man different from the boy who had started out to college, different also from what he had been three years before. There was, at twenty-six, a tiredness about him, a diminishment of the self-confidence that had set him apart from the herd. He was grimly aloof now, silent and unapproachable.

Those who knew him speculated about it. It was said that he was that way because he had worked himself nearly to death to get through medical school. He was tired out; but he would get over it in time.

It was said that he'd been set to marry a girl named Gloria who'd jilted him for another because she didn't want to be a small-town doctor's wife. But it was best she had, if she was that kind; and he would get over it in time.

It was said that he was grieving because his grandfather was ailing badly and was surely fixing to die soon.

Esther heard what was said and suffered with him. She went to him the first week that he was home and said, "I came because we're old friends, Joe. I'd like to help you if I could. You're going to need money to set up your practice and I've been saving since I started working. I could make you a loan and you could pay me back after you got on your feet."

Her voice and manner were business-like. But he scowled and answered sharply, "Thanks. But I don't need it. Dr. Mitchell has loaned me the money."

She remembered that Dr. Mitchell was the one who had been kind to Joe as a boy. It pleased her to know that he had kept in touch with him over the years. Evidently the old doctor's initial interest and confidence in the boy had endured, since he was lending him the money now.

As if reading her thoughts, Joe said, "I didn't ask him. He offered. In any event, I couldn't borrow from you, Esther."

She left it at that, and afterwards she avoided him, as he avoided her. She knew it was painful for him to see her now.

The contrast between them was too obvious: he so gaunt and shabby, with his career not yet begun, while she had never looked so well. And she had already made a name for herself. South Leemouth regarded Miss Kennedy, the colored supervisor of nurses at Wharton Memorial Annex, with much respect; for wasn't she responsible for the change in that hell hole to a fit place to go when you were sick?

Although the fine new building, miracle that it was, was said to be some of Miss Kennedy's doings, no one knew for sure. But it was the change in morale that people talked about most—the difference in the way the nurses treated the patients, in the way they treated each other. That, everyone knew for sure, was because of Miss Kennedy's influence. And South Leemouth was proud.

When the new annex was completed, a woman's club voted Esther their Woman of the Year. She was asked to lecture to various civic and church groups. She had even been called upon to deliver a commencement address at her former high school.

Only Miss Head, sensing the frustration in her, said gently one day, "I know you feel even this hasn't been enough. My dear girl, I don't think you realize what a step forward the new building is!"

"I realize it," Esther said.

"Tell me, Esther, how did you manage it?"

"Manage what, Miss Head?"

"To get the Board of Directors to allocate the funds. I know you'll never admit it. But you did have a hand in it somewhere. Somehow I know you did!"

Esther smiled. "You overestimate me. What influence could a colored woman have over the Board of Directors?"

"That will worry me to my grave!" Miss Head declared. She changed the subject. "Anyway, now that this is accomplished, what more do you want?"

"For there to be no need for an annex at all!"

Miss Head, not liking it, understood it. She said drily, "Till then, just continue to do your best."

Joe, informed of Esther's respected position in the community, commended her on a note of sarcasm. "You've made quite a name for yourself around here, I hear."

This came on the heels of his refusal to accept money from her. She saw in his eyes the hurt to his pride struggling with his pride in her, and she lashed herself for not having foreseen how he'd feel. She should not have gone to him with the offer of her aid. But she would let him alone now for both their sakes. She never saw him that she wasn't overcome with the quick, deep tenderness, the memory of their passion, and the hunger to be in his arms again. In fact, every meeting was for both of them a struggle between heart and will.

"He tears me up," Esther said bleakly to Munsie one day.

"No more'n you tear him up," Munsie replied. "At least, let that be some comfort to you. Ain't no fun to love by yourself."

It was strangely easier for Esther to confide in Munsie since she knew of her secret passion for Sam, although they never spoke of that.

"It's not love Joe feels for me," Esther answered wryly. "Something more like bitterness. Poor Joe! He does have bad luck with his women."

"If you's talking about that Gloria they say he was fixing to marry, seems to me it wasn't so much love as to show you he could get along without you. Men are generally stupid, Esther. You just got to hold on till they see the light. Anyway, how come you don't try to forget Joe, and give some thought to some of these other fellows come around? Now, that farm demonstration agent looks a likely man to me. And he's colleged, ain't he?"

"I've tried, but Munsie, none of them is . . ." Esther looked helplessly at her friend.

"None of them is Joe, eh?" Munsie looked sad and wise. "Women sure do have a hard row to hoe."

Munsie was right, of course. Esther knew that it was time to start thinking about marriage. But her heart would accept no substitute for Joe, even though she felt the need of a husband. More than that, even though Hope needed a father.

While their mothers were talking in the kitchen, Hope and Ishmael were having their own conversation in the back yard.

"I don't know what's the matter with you any more," Hope said. "You used to didn't mind playing house with me." She stuck a careless angry finger into one mild eye of the doll that had come to her on her eighth birthday.

"That's for girls," Ish said reproachfully. "And for little boys. How'd it look, me playing with dolls, and eleven years old? We could play some marbles though," he added, to lessen the risk of displeasing her.

She shook her brown curls vigorously. "No. I'll just play alone, since you're so mean!"

"Suit yourself." He shrugged, but his eyes were anxious. After a silence he said, "She's a pretty doll. Looks almost like a real baby."

Hope regarded him silently for a moment, and then dimpled engagingly. "You hold her while I fix her bottle."

He had no choice, for she thrust the doll at him; and he held it helplessly while she did female things with a miniature stove and pot and bottle. Ishmael sighed. No matter what the issue, Hope always won. He ought to let her alone and go find some boys to play with. He never knew how it was she held him. But he was entranced by her—her golden face with its shifting expressions, her mercurial moods, her complete acceptance of him as belonging to her. He only knew that she provoked him and, by some magic, delighted him.

"I'll bet I know something you don't," she said, repossessing the doll.

"Yes? What?"

"I know how babies come."

He frowned. "Who told you?"

"Why, Mama did!" She laughed. "I asked her."

"You're kidding!"

"No, I'm not. She said they come out of the mother. She told me a lot more, too." One brown wing of an eyebrow shot up teasingly as she estimated the effect of her news. "You mean you didn't know that!"

"Of course I knew, silly. Long ago. And I didn't have to ask my mother either."

"How come?"

"Boys know things sooner than girls, that's all."

Surprisingly, she nodded at that. "I think so too." She laid the doll on the ground carelessly and regarded him with serious hazel eyes. "Ish, what's a bastard?"

He frowned again. "How come you ask that? Where'd you hear that word, Hope?"

"In school. A boy called another boy that, and Miss Roberts sent him to the principal. What's a bastard?"

He lowered his eyes. "I don't know."

"You're a big story. You do too know."

"Well, why don't you ask your Mama?"

" 'Cause it's a bad word. I know that much. I just don't know what it means, that's all."

He was silent.

"I won't speak to you again until you tell me." Hope always threatened in calm tones. And she was as calm about carrying out the threat.

"I think it means when somebody's father and mother aren't married," he said uncomfortably.

She nodded, pulling her lips to a point, a way she had when thoughtful. "I thought so."

"I thought you said you didn't know."

"Ish, am I a bastard?"

For a long moment their eyes held. He said, his voice rising helplessly, "How would I know? No more than me, I guess. It's a bad word. You oughtn't to use it."

She went suddenly deathly pale, and her eyes were brilliant in her face. "Then I am a bastard!"

"No, Hope. I didn't say that. Oh, Lord, you do mix me up! So what if your father and mother ain't never been married? Mine ain't neither. It does us no harm, does it?"

Her face crumpled and she began to cry. "I don't know. Everybody else's father and mother are married!"

He took out his handkerchief and, finding a clean corner, began to wipe her tears as they came. "Don't cry, Hope. It's not worth crying about. I'm sorry I told you. Me 'n' my big mouth!"

She sobbed harder.

He said anxiously, "Aunt Essie ever finds out I told you, she'll skin me alive."

She lifted her wet convulsed face wonderingly. "But I won't tell her. I wouldn't tell on you. Besides, she's supposed to tell me."

He was startled. She was too young to figure things out like that.

"Did your mother tell you yet?" Hope asked.

"No. Don't suppose she will. Guess she knows I know by now, anyway."

"Did you cry when you found out?" she asked softly.

He didn't answer. They stared at each other miserably; but deeper than their misery was the comfort in the knowledge that it was mutual.

Chapter Twenty-eight

DESPITE A general pride in there being at last a colored doctor in South Leemouth, Negroes there had some reservations about being the first to patronize young Dr. Mead. There was, in the first place, a natural reluctance because of his youth and inexperience. There was, additionally, the never acknowledged but deep-rooted suspicion that white doctors surely had better training and skill. It was hard to trust something so important as the curing of sickness to someone who hadn't yet earned a reputation as a doctor. It was better to let others try him out first. So with some secret shame, most of South Leemouth stayed away from the small office on Proctor Street and went, as usual, to the white doctors in Leemouth.

Those that did go were the very poor, who figured that this doctor would be more patient about waiting for his fee; the very old, who figured they'd die anyway; and the very race-minded who prided themselves on their valor. But he gave to these his best services, his patient, grave, confident manner, as if they were all he asked. And it was said of him that he was a good doctor, skilled, serious, and kind. Still people waited for time to prove the truth of the rumor.

Esther bled for him. She'd see him coming home at night, walking from the bus stop, letting his fatigue and discouragement show because he thought no one was looking. And he would go home to the shabby little house opposite, to try to cheer an aging and ill Pa Mead. And each day her concern for him grew. At the risk of her job, she began slyly to browbeat some of the more prosperous patients in the annex.

"Mrs. Foster, I don't know why you didn't have Dr. Mead treat your palpitations when they first started. He's a real wonder with heart cases, you know."

"No, I didn't know. Is that a fact? Maybe I ought to see him after I get out."

"Mrs. Lacey, you ought to take that girl of yours to Dr. Mead. He knows all about acne. I bet he'll have it cleared up in no time!"

"You know a neighbor of mine had a bad attack of bursitis just like yours, Mrs. Willingham, and Dr. Mead cured her in two days! After you get those tonsils out, why don't you see him?"

It was easy enough, if less than ethical. People who would not take the word of others were willing to believe the supervisor of nurses. During all the months that followed in which Esther dropped her broad hints, she prayed for two things: that Joe, the doctor, would merit her faith in him; and that she wouldn't be called on the carpet for what she was doing.

"If you ask me, you're sticking your neck way out," Munsie said when Esther confided her worries to her. "And it don't seem to me he deserves it. Girl, you sure do have that ever-living love!"

"Oh, shut up!" Esther said.

Esther didn't like the idea that she was something of a meddler; but she couldn't seem to help herself where people she loved were concerned. She had long been concerned about the relationship between Lucy and Sam, and one day while visiting with her sister the suggestion just seemed to make itself.

"Lucy, why don't you try to have a baby?"

Lucy stopped her machine to frown at her. "What you trying to do now—hurt my feelings?"

"You know I didn't mean it like that."

"Well, I ain't done nothing to keep from having children. I guess the Lord just ain't seen fit."

Having gone so far, Esther couldn't let it lie there. "It's not the Lord's fault. If you and Sam really want children, at least you could find out why you haven't had any. It could be just some little thing that's holding you back."

"You mean in me, or Sam?" Lucy's voice was suspicious.

"It could be either, or both, or neither. At least, if you went to a doctor you could be sure. And if there's something that could be done, he could do it and you could have your baby."

Behind the belligerence, there was a wistfulness in Lucy's eyes. "And what doctor are you suggesting? Not Joe?"

Esther wanted to giggle. For once she hadn't thought of promoting Joe. Still it was another opportunity. "Why not Joe?" she asked seriously, lowering her eyes. "He's a good doctor."

"He ain't no woman doctor. Just a g. p."

"Which doesn't mean he can't take care of a case like this. Besides, Joe would give you more attention and sympathy than all the white doctors put together."

"I don't like the idea of Joe poking up in me. Don't seem right, seeing we're friends an' all. It would embarrass me, Esther." Her voice grew unexpectedly mild and shy.

Esther was touched. She said, "You wouldn't have to go to Joe, dear. Dr. Matthews is awfully good. And I'd go with you whenever you want. But maybe you'd better let Sam go first. It could be him, you know."

"I'd be shamed to ask Sam to do that."

"I'd talk to him if you want me to. Sam and I are old friends, and sometimes sisters-in-law can say things wives can't." She said it lightly, and was happy to see the smile dawn on Lucy's face.

"Esther, you sure I'm not too old?"

"At twenty-six? Don't be silly. If everything works out, you'll just have to watch out not to have one right after another."

And Lucy was suddenly radiant. Esther always held her breath when she saw her sister so. At rare times Lucy was capable of being totally lovely. But it was always a fleeting thing, and it didn't last now.

"I don't know about it, Esther. Maybe it ain't right to meddle with the Lord's will."

Esther said nothing.

"And even so, supposing after all the expense and everything it wasn't no good. Supposing—"

She broke off abruptly. She stared at Esther a moment and then thrust aside the sewing to get up and move to the kitchen with rapid steps. "I better start the dinner now. Sam'll be home soon. You'll excuse me, Esther."

Hope was in the garden, lying on her stomach on the grass, absorbed in her book. Esther stood at the gate watching her. She stood motionless to lengthen the moment or two before Hope would feel her gaze and look up, trying as she looked at her child to understand what she hadn't understood before—that no matter what she said to the contrary, in her deepest heart Lucy did not want a child of her own.

It was not her obvious fear of childbirth that Esther found incomprehensible. It was the deeper and darker fear that being a mother would mean a total involvement with and responsibility for another human being. It was that that had been in Lucy's face as she made her desperate excuses. And seeing it, Esther had fled from her with the same wild instinct that had awakened her as a child from a dark and tortured nightmare.

Now in the bright August sunlight, by the familiar garden gate, Esther was touched to pity. Barring an act of God, Lucy would have no child. She would nibble at motherhood through her relationship with Hope; use it to satisfy her conscience or whatever maternal instinct she had.

True, Lucy had been anxious enough to adopt Hope, the four-year-old, when the child had been a cute and clinging possession. But Hope at eight, with her developing independence, her probing questions, her uncertain temperament, was too bewildering to Lucy. She was glad now that Hope was Esther's and not hers. She would retain her affection for Hope unless it burdened her too greatly, in which case she could dispense with it. Was there a danger to Hope in that, Esther wondered.

Hope discovered her presence. "Hi, Mama!" she said.

The child's bright face was a reassurance. "What're you reading, Hope?"

"A book Tattie bought me. It's good. Mama, can I have hamburger for dinner?"

"Sure, Honey. You may also have spinach."

Esther laughed, and winked at her offspring as she went

inside. Hope would spend the next hour figuring a way to avoid having spinach with her hamburger. She was like that. She was Paul's child.

Chapter Twenty-nine

"How LONG more I got to stay here, Esther?"

It was still an effort for Pa to speak; for since the stroke that had brought him to the hospital his tongue was unwieldy. "'Twon't obey my mind," he'd labor to explain to the doctor, the nurse, and the visitor, for he was embarrassed at the attentive patience his illness inflicted on others, embarrassed that his paralyzed right side made him dependent on them.

He repeated the question.

"Don't you worry about that now, darling," Esther said gently.

He had been there six months, and she had visited with him every day, even on her off days. Always he asked the same anxious question.

"Must he a big expense on Joe," Pa said sadly out of his twisted mouth.

"He can afford it, Pa." Esther was sorry for Pa's sake that she said it shortly.

"He's coming today?" Pa's voice was not hopeful.

"I don't know. He's very busy, you know."

"Yes. He's a good doctor, ain't he?" And there was a sad pride in the old eyes.

"A very good doctor." She changed the subject and began to talk of Hope and her progress at school, forcing herself to be natural and cheerful. It wouldn't do for Pa to see that the very mention of Joe infuriated her.

In two short years, Joe had built his practice from nothing to one that vied in numbers with the best white doctors in Leemouth. At first Esther had been elated over his success. She didn't know when she first began to realize the changes it made in him. There were the obvious things that she hadn't immediately noticed or thought important. If he began to be a bit flashy, to wear expensive suits and drive a high-powered car, it was right that he should enjoy the fruits of his labors. If there were rumors that he was getting to be something of a gay dog with the ladies—especially, it seemed, among the schoolteachers, he was after all the most eligible young Negro in town, and that was to be expected. That was none of her concern, Esther told herself.

She had found excuses for him as he gradually cut himself away from his old intimates, having little to do with the neighbors, even less with Sam and Lucy. But that he could find it in his heart to shun his own grandfather was unthinkable.

One day, before the old man suffered the stroke, Esther had been leaving the Mead house as Joe was coming in. She said, carefully because the new Joe was a stranger to her, "Joe, Pa shouldn't be left alone so much. The neighbors do their best in the day, but the evenings are long for him. He's sick and he's lonesome. Couldn't you try to—"

He had cut her short. "Esther, I do the best I can. I'm so busy nowadays I don't have time for myself. I know it's pretty grim around here. But soon as I'm out of my financial woods, I'll be able to fix up the place and hire a housekeeper."

He saw her wry expression and added defensively, "I know what you're going to say. But the car was necessary, and a doctor must dress decently, and I haven't finished paying off Dr. Mitchell yet."

She said in exasperation, "Joe, I'm not talking about your spending money! I'm talking about your neglecting that sick old man who took you in when you had nowhere else to go, and raised you and cared for you the best he could! Now he's so proud of you because of your success as a doctor. But as a person you're letting him down. You're acting as if you're ashamed of him!"

There was a quickly banished flicker of pain in his expression. He said sardonically, "People I've loved have let me down all my life. I guess I'm no better than the next, Esther." And he turned abruptly away from her and went inside.

For a while after Pa suffered the stroke and was hospitalized in the annex, Joe appeared more subdued, genuinely concerned because of the old man's brush with death. But as the months wore on, with Pa rallying slowly, Joe's visits grew shorter, less frequent. And the grandfather pined, but inwardly, never condemning nor complaining, asking only his daily question, "How long more I got to stay here?" —thinking bewilderedly that he wouldn't feel so outcast and forgotten in his own familiar home. "Not that folks ain't nice here," he'd hasten to add. And it was true that he was the darling of the annex, petted and spoiled by the nurses; but he pined nonetheless. And there were times when Esther almost hated Joe Mead.

Pa wasn't really listening now to her news about Hope,

and he was tiring. She kissed his cheek and told him that she'd see him tomorrow.

He looked apologetic. "Hope—how old now?" he had learned to be sparing with words since they came with such difficulty.

"Ten next birthday. She's grown so you wouldn't know her. She sent you a kiss." She delivered it, and he smiled wearily and took her hand with his good left one.

"You're a good girl. Your Grandear—proud." His old eyes peered at her pleadingly. "Joe's good too. Just young. Ain't he?"

Why was he making her say it, she wondered. She said it. "Yes, Pa. Joe's a good boy."

The following Saturday, Hope suggested to Esther that they have their lunch on the hill. Esther hid her surprise. Hope seldom wanted to go there any more. She had acquired a small coterie of intimate girl friends, characteristically older than her ten years, and was usually satisfied playing with them. The hill was reserved for special conferences with her mother: to wheedle for a certain new dress or a favor—the last time it had been for a bicycle—or to charm Esther out of her annoyance over a bad report card.

Esther had learned to be firm on such occasions. She was determined not to let her daughter grow up thinking that everything could be had or be put right by charm. Hope admired her mother's attitude while she deplored it, and had been heard to say to her friends with some pride that her mother was the only adult she knew who couldn't be "coaxed out of things."

For all her firmness, Esther took much pride in Hope. She was proud of the child's swift, keen intellect, of her undeviating honesty—Hope never lied—of her impulse to charity that made her kind to the aged and the unfortunate, of the loyalty that had kept the hill still a secret. Hope never took anyone else there, although Esther had not forbidden it. Esther knew that sometimes she went alone, and she wondered what Hope thought of then and what she did there. But she didn't ask, for it was native to Esther not to invade the privacy of others.

She packed a special lunch, and they went to the hill and ate it quietly, not conversing much. Hope seemed preoccupied, and Esther waited for her to say what was on her mind. She said it finally, without preamble or emphasis. "I want you to tell me about my father."

"Yes," Esther said. "I'll tell you whatever you want to know."

There was a silence in which Hope pulled her knees up to her chin, and inspected her mother's face.

"He was white, wasn't he, Mama?"

"Yes, Hope, he was. How'd you know?"

"I don't know. I guessed it a long time ago."

"Why didn't you ask me before?"

"I was waiting till you told me." There was some accusation in her tone.

Esther, outwardly calm, said, "I haven't been trying to hide things from you, Hope. But I didn't want to force them on you either. I was waiting till you asked me."

"Well, who was he? I mean, what's his name?"

"Paul Miller. He lives over in Leemouth and works at the First Savings Bank."

"You ever see him?" Hope's gaze was intent.

"Very seldom."

"You speak to each other when you do?"

"Yes, we do. At least we say how do you do."

She absorbed that. "Mama, were you and he in love?"

Esther's pulse quickened. She took her time about answering. "Hope, we were drawn to each other. We were very young and we didn't give much thought to how things are down here."

The child's eyes widened. "But Mama! Everybody knows how things are down here. You must have known black can't marry white!"

Esther said gravely, "We knew."

"Then you were really in love!" It was an entreaty, a statement of hoped-for fact.

"I wouldn't be honest if I said that, Hope. All I can tell you is that your father, as I knew him, was a nice young man and I liked him."

Hope's face wore a queer little smile, but Esther didn't see it. She was praying fervently that her explanation would be enough; for how could she say to her daughter that her father had raped her?

"Mama, could I go to the bank to see him sometime?"

Esther had anticipated the question. She steeled herself and said, "Hope, your father doesn't know about you. I never told him. I didn't want him to know, and don't now."

She waited while Hope's eyes grew dark and unfathomable. After a while, the girl spoke. "Then I don't really have a father, do I, Mama?"

Esther yearned to hold her. "No, Hope. Not really. All along I've tried to do what's best for you. I hope you'll trust me. I know it's hard. I never knew my father either, even though he and my mother were married."

"It's not the same thing," Hope said. And Esther had to agree.

"Couldn't I just go to look at him once? I wouldn't say anything. I wouldn't even let him know I'm looking."

And because there was no way to stop that from happening eventually, Esther agreed.

The next time that she had to go to the bank, Esther took Hope with her. She hoped that Paul would be visible there, because she didn't want to have to repeat the ordeal.

Hope was tense and quiet on the bus. As they entered the bank Esther said, "If he's here, I'll point him out to you. Try to act normally." Hope looked at her shrewdly and told her not to worry.

Paul was standing at the counter talking to one of the tellers. Seeing him though Hope's eyes, Esther thought with some dismay how handsome and cultivated he looked.

"He's over there on your right, behind the counter. The one with the grey suit and blond hair."

He hadn't seen her, for which Esther was grateful. Hope separated herself from her and went to sit on one of the benches beneath the palms along the wall. The child was clever. If Paul caught her staring, he wouldn't associate her with Esther.

Esther took her time about making her deposits. She wouldn't bring Hope again; but since they were there, she wanted to make sure she gave her every chance.

Hope made no comment on the way home. Later, she said, "He's important, isn't he? He was telling that man what to do."

"Yes, he's important at the bank. He's a vice-president now."

"Mama, I'm what you'd call half-white, aren't I?"

Esther decided not to be technical. "Yes, although I don't like the term." She looked at her daughter and was shocked that in the hazel eyes was a glimmer of pride. "You're half-Negro too, Hope," she said sternly. "And don't you forget it!"

Then she thought that what she'd said only served to further confuse the child, to further obscure her sense of identity. So she said, "Hope, the important thing is not to forget that you're you, a whole individual person. . . ."

She stopped, because she sounded pompous, and because Hope wasn't listening anyway.

Chapter Thirty

PA MEAD suffered another stroke on a Sunday afternoon in late September and died the same day. The nurse who was with him said that his last words were, "Joe! Where's Joe?"

But Joe, who hadn't visited the old man for two days, wasn't to be found until it was too late. And then he was discovered in a little highway café, drinking and dancing with some unidentified girl. And South Leemouth held it against him.

At the funeral, he sat bowed and still while people passed him to pay their silent, and often tearful, respect to the dead. The Reverend Billingsley preached what was for him a subdued sermon, saying that for him this death was a personal sorrow, dwelling on Pa's virtues as a neighbor, a friend, a family man, and a citizen, but never once calling Joe by name.

Esther wept for the loss of Pa, but as much for Joe. When she made to go to him afterwards, Munsie took her arm. "Now ain't the time, Esther."

"But he needs me."

"That's why it ain't the time," Munsie said ambiguously.

At the cemetery, Munsie went herself to stand near the young doctor. Sam followed, and Lucy. Esther stayed at the opposite side with Hope and Ishmael. But as the casket was lowered into the grave, Joe lifted his eyes to look at her. The tears were streaming down his cheeks unashamedly; and she left the children, forcing her way over to him, to take his hand, to hold it until it was all over. He held tightly to the hand she gave. But, the ceremony done, he broke away from her without saying a word.

Later, at Esther's house, Munsie explained. "I didn't want you to go to him, because I know how proud he is. And I thought he might hurt your feelings—tell you to let him alone or something."

"The thing I don't understand," Lucy said, "is how you can care so much for him after he has shown everybody how he is."

Sam turned patient rebuking eyes on his wife. "Lucy, don't you know yet that folks don't love because of. They loves in spite of!"

Things might not have gone as they did if Joe hadn't decided immediately after the funeral to tear down the old Mead house and build a new one. It was, to the citizens of South Leemouth, a gesture of defiance. If the doctor had shown remorse, they would have been willing to forgive. But he was still seen after office hours dancing and drinking in out-of-the-way cafés. And he stayed away from his old neighbors entirely, now that he'd torn down the house. Folks said he was rooming with one of his schoolteacher friends. The destruction of his grandfather's house meant that he was just waiting all along for the old man to die to get the property. It was heartless and callous, and who could trust a man like that? "He won't do it on my money!" people were heard to say. And his patients began to seek out their original physicians. Joe's practice, that a few months before had witnessed so spectacular a rise, now began as meteoric a fall.

There came a day in the middle of winter, when the workmen stopped work on the Mead house and never went back. People said that it was because the doctor didn't have any more money to pay them. In fact, it was a wonder if he had any money at all, because his office was empty nearly all the time now. And it served him right.

Esther worried for him, and grew thin and irritable because she was powerless to help him. Then one night he came to her out of the rain. She opened the door and found him there, wet to the skin, his eyes wild and hunted.

They stood looking at each other with the wind whistling through the open door, and the rain streaking across the porch floor.

He said, at last, "Thou art the blood of my heart of hearts. Help me, Esther."

And she opened her arms and took him in.

Chapter Thirty-one

THERE WAS a big to-do in the papers about Paul Miller's marriage to Cynthia Hamilton, and Esther was sorry because it made it a doubly hard time for Hope. Hope, surprisingly, hadn't taken kindly to the idea of her mother marrying Joe Mead. She had said, in apparently utter amazement, "But Mama! What you want to do that for?"

"Because I love him, darling. And he loves me."

The child's expression was pained. "But you can't! I mean —well, Mama, are you sure you're not thinking I need a father? I don't, you know. I mean you don't have to marry somebody on my account."

Esther stared at the small troubled face. Hope was saying that she wanted no substitute father—only her own, for she had seen the man from whose loins she had come and was ensnared by him. Esther understood this yearning, for it had been hers. *Lucy and Esther are sorry their Papa died.*

She took her child in her arms and tried to speak calmly. "Hope, don't you like Joe? Haven't you always called him your Jojo?"

"I like him all right. But I don't know why you want to marry him."

"Because I need a husband. Not just any husband. I need Joe. You see, I've always loved him."

Hope broke away and there was a great fury in her eyes. "You can't! You're lying to me! You can't love him like you loved my father!" And she ran sobbing out of the house.

A week later, the papers carried the news of Paul's marriage. Esther read the account in the morning paper at the hospital. "A brilliant match," the *Star* said, "joining two of Leemouth's most influential families." There were pictures of Cynthia, more beautiful than Esther remembered, and of Paul, more handsome. She read in his face that he had put away his youthful rebellions, had set his feet in the family mold. But those two were still the same. Theirs would be a rocky way.

But that was not Esther's concern. There was Hope, who would see the pictures and the story in the afternoon paper before she got home. Hope read the funnies in the paper every day. That afternoon, when Esther inspected the paper, a page was missing. She decided to say nothing about it. Nor did Hope. Not then or later. But they both knew that the other knew, and there was strain between them, and a breach that Esther could find no way of mending.

"She has some idea that her father and I were star-crossed lovers," she said to Joe, "and nothing I can say seems to shake her from it. Now with his marrying Cynthia and me marrying you, she's pretty confused. Maybe we ought to wait, Joe."

"Will we really help her by waiting?"

"I don't know. I don't know what to do about her." She looked at him helplessly, quickened to tears by the miraculous open tenderness in his face. Whenever she saw him now, she thought of the passage describing the Prodigal Son: "And when he came to himself . . ."

He drew her close, and rubbed his chin gently along her forehead, talking into her hair. "I understand her, you know.

She's following my pattern. If the things and the people we love most aren't the way we want them, we decide we won't have them at all. Something makes us want to punish them and ourselves. Esther, up to two weeks ago, I was an unmitigated ass, and it's a miracle that you've loved me through it all."

She put her hand to his mouth. "Don't. We aren't going to talk about it."

He gave a small chuckle. "Why? You've only to look across the way at Joe Mead's Folly, as my half-finished house is called, to know I was an ass. All right! What I'm saying is, I went along feeling life had given me a pretty raw deal, and I was real busy striking back—boomerang blows—hurting other people, you, Pa, a few girls along the way, but mostly myself."

She tightened her arms about him, moving her body to fit his. He held her, but kept his mouth out of reach. "No, you little devil. Let me finish. Esther, no matter what I did, I always loved you, always wanted you. But I was too proud, too hurt, I thought, to come to you. I'm ashamed that when I did, it was in my despair and my failure and my guilt. But when I came, it was because I knew that this thing, this one good thing we've always had between us, was the one thing that could put the pieces back together. I thought, humbly, darling, hopefully, maybe you had a few pieces that needed mending too."

She said, "I did, Joe. I do. I've never been whole without you."

He lifted her chin with his finger, his dark almond-shaped eyes searching hers. "Then, if we're whole together, wouldn't we have a better chance of helping Hope to be whole too? I do love her, you know, Esther."

She pulled his mouth to hers for an answer.

They were married by the Reverend Sylvester Billingsley in Ebenezer Baptist Church on a Friday evening. There were no guests besides the family and Munsie and Ishmael. After the ceremony, Rev. Billingsley said in his ponderous way, "I've watched you two grow since you was children. I know your grandparents are smiling in heaven this day. You've made your young mistakes. But now you's fully grown and can help each other. I pray you will walk the rest of your earthly journey together in love and joy."

They thanked him. Munsie was crying joyfully. Sam, who had given the bride away, said to Hope, "Kiss your Mama and your new Daddy, Hope, and wish them happiness."

Hope, dutifully and quietly, did as she was told. She

kept her eyes lowered as she said, "I wish you happiness, Mama." But when she spoke to Joe, she looked full at her mother. "I wish you happiness, Joe." And her eyes were defiant and anguished.

At the same moment, Esther caught Lucy's expression, a while before sullen, now satanically amused.

Chapter Thirty-two

THE FOLLOWING two years were happy ones for Esther and Joe. They were less so for Lucy and Sam.

Sam Adams was a man who took life as it came. Few dreams had been born in him in his lifetime, and those few were simple ones, capable of being realized. He had chosen Lucy as a wife and won her. It never occurred to him to question this choice that had made him less than happy. Lucy was what she was, and there was no help for it. That she bore him no children, that she gave him little warmth or tenderness, was the hand of fate; and it was not in Sam's nature to cry out at fate.

Sam did not dream foolishly of what might have been. But after many years of marriage, he discovered in himself a vague hunger, a gnawing knowledge that he was less than fulfilled. And after much thinking about it, he decided that what he was hankering for was a car. He did not see in this a desire for freedom, for escape from the empty routine of his life with Lucy. He saw only that he wanted a car, and he was determined to have it.

He set about obtaining it by the simple process of saving for it. Lucy, who had grown more and more frugal through the years and who handled all the money, would not be partial to the idea of putting her carefully accrued savings into a car, and Sam knew it. When he was given a raise of five dollars a week on his job, Sam, for the first time in his life, resorted to guile. He neglected to mention the raise to Lucy, and for two years he saved the additional money until he had five hundred dollars.

His small deception would have gone on indefinitely, had he not one day chanced upon a beautiful little coupe, only three years old, and selling for the incredibly low sum of eight hundred dollars. He stood in the used car lot looking at it for an hour. Then he went home to stand up to Lucy.

"Lucy, we been married thirteen years now, and I ain't never asked nothing for myself. Every week I gives you my money to spend as you see fit. All I ask is three hundred now for a little old second-hand car."

"We ain't got it," Lucy said shortly.

Sam lost his temper. "You damn well *do* got it! You got more'n six thousand in the bank now!"

"Which took me thirteen years to save. I don't want no car nohow! Besides, can't be much of a car for three hundred dollars."

He said hastily, "It's in good condition, but that ain't the point. It'll keep me from having to stand out in the rain and cold waiting for a bus to go to work. I do thinks I deserve that much, Lucy. You'd still have lots of money in the bank. What you saving so hard for anyhow?"

She looked at him acidly. "If I was fixing to buy anything, I'd get me some new furniture in here. This old stuff is falling apart. But I got sense enough to know I can't compete with folks like the Meads, who have got themselves a new living-room suit."

Sam looked at her wonderingly. "You ain't never gonna quit being jealous of Esther, is you?"

"That ain't true, Sam Adams! But since you mention it, ain't no reason she can have things I can't. They ain't been married but two years. After thirteen years, I ought to have some of the things I want, too."

Sam pounded his big fist on the table. "Ain't I always taken care of you, Lucy? Thirteen years I've climbed scaffolds and hammered nails in the wet and the cold, so's you could stay out of the white woman's kitchen. What you makes with your sewing don't keep this house, you know! I done the best I could, and if it ain't fancy like your sister got now, it's because you's married to a carpenter, not a doctor!"

"Don't I know that!" Lucy's voice dripped sarcasm.

He was not to be interrupted. "I love you. Lord knows why, 'cause you got some mean ways. You so jealous of Esther with Joe, now he's getting back on his feet—"

"Ain't that the only reason he married her? So's he could get back on his feet? 'Twas on her account folks started using him for their doctor again. And he's living in her house, and she's still working. She ain't got it so hot, if you ask me." Lucy seldom followed a logical pattern of reasoning.

Sam gave up that tack. He said more placatingly, "Look, Lucy. Don't let's quarrel. Just let me have the money."

She looked at him thoughtfully. "Sam, I don't mean to be hard on you. You been a good husband to me. But this ain't no time to be dipping in our savings."

"Why not?"

She raised her eyes to his, and in them was some pride

and much fear. " 'Cause we're going to have a baby, Sam."
Then she was crying, great tears rolling down her cheeks.

For a moment he said nothing in his astonishment. Then
his face stretched into a wide joyous grin. He went to her
and took her awkwardly in his arms. "Honey, you're sure?"

She nodded, still sobbing into his shoulder. "I went to Dr.
Matthews. Three months."

"Then why're you crying, Lucy? That's great! After all
these years! Oh, Honey! Oh, Honey!"

She looked up at him, blinking the rapidly flowing tears
away to see his face. "I'm scared. I want the baby. But oh,
Lord, I'm scared! I'm thirty-one, Sam, and I always been
sickly . . ."

He rocked her in his big arms, like a child, and he crooned,
"Don't be scared, Honey. We'll get you the best. I'll work
my fingers to the nub so you can have the best. So don't cry
now. Don't cry."

But to Sam, giving birth was no great wonder. It was a
natural part of living. His mother had had eleven. As he
soothed his wife, he was thinking that there was still no
reason why he shouldn't have the car. Perhaps he could
borrow the money from Esther and Joe. He could pay them
back five dollars a week.

As Lucy intended she should, Hope delivered the news at
home. Hope had a sense of drama and waited until dinner
was almost over and they were having coffee. Then she
said casually, "Jojo, what would Tattie and Uncle Sam's
child be to me?"

"Your cousin. Why, sweetheart?"

"I just wondered, so I'll know what to call it when it gets
here."

Esther set her cup down with a clatter. "Hope, did your
Aunt Lucy tell you she was going to have a baby?"

"Sure. Didn't you know? She's three months, and she's
going to Dr. Matthews."

"Good Lord!" Esther breathed.

"I thought that'd floor you." Hope said with satisfaction.
"Jojo, can I have an extra dollar tomorrow?"

They were friends now. Hope steadfastly refused to call
him Daddy, although she had consented to the legal adop-
tion that changed her name to Mead. Esther was grateful
for the good relationship, such as it was, that had grown
between her husband and child. Joe was patient and tact-
ful with Hope, but firm. Hope, in her turn, with her philoso-
phy of winning flies with honey, was affectionate with him,
and only occasionally disobedient. But she never thought of

him as her father, and Esther knew it, and some small part of her grieved because of it.

"What's the dollar for?" Joe wanted to know.

"We're making a surprise gift to the teacher. She's been pretty nice, helping with the slow students and all."

"Okay. You'd better get to your homework now, young lady."

"Sure." Hope stood up and tossed her thick brown pony-tail, a recent gesture that was part of her rapidly advancing adolescence. "Mama, if you see Ish at the hospital tomorrow, ask him how he enjoyed taking Wilma Cummings to the movies. Tell him I heard about it." She winked at her mother.

"So what do you care?" Esther asked, amused. "You treat him like dirt. And if he's old enough to be an attendant at the hospital, he's old enough to take a girl to the movies."

"Your time'll come, Miss," Joe said. "Give it a couple of years. You're just twelve."

"Oh, you two!" Hope pouted. "Who cares? I just want to tease him. He's always pretending he hasn't a girl. As for me, I've better fish to fry. When you decide to let me go to the movies with a boy, it won't be with Ishmael Atwater, you can bet!"

"You could do worse." Joe laughed. "Ish will be a fine doctor one of these days. I have a feeling about him."

"He has a feeling about you too," Hope retorted. "Hero worship like mad! All he can say is, Joe this and Joe that. Honestly, it's sickening!"

They laughed together as she left the room. Esther turned to her husband. "Lucy having a baby! Joe, you think this'll make her happy?"

"Why not? When're you going to do that for me, Friend?"

"We can go to bed and start now," Esther answered light-ly. And desire rose and leapt between them, causing them both to tremble and move towards each other.

He reached for her, but she broke away, laughing. "Dishes first. We're old marrieds now, remember?"

But later that night they would lie together till the dawn broke. And Esther sang softly as she did the dishes. She fought sometimes with this man she had married, for each was strong, independent, and passionate. But there were quiet tender moments between them, and sudden unbidden nights like this, wildly surrendered to their single primitive need, and the mornings after that were holy.

Sunday afternoon, Esther had Sam and Lucy to dinner in

honor of their anticipated parenthood. Lucy was indeed rounder, and Esther wondered why she hadn't noticed it before. She also seemed happy, proud of her accomplishment, proud of Sam, and therefore kinder to everyone. When Hope teased her that she would love her less when the baby was born, Lucy protested with great concern, "That's ridiculous. I'll always love you, Baby. I've raised you as much as your mother has!" Hope, in her impulsive way, rewarded her with a loud kiss. And Esther was pleased that many tensions had eased for the whole family.

Munsie had been invited to the dinner, but had begged off. "Esther, it ain't that I ain't happy for them. God knows I am! Especially for Sam. It's just that—well, right along in here, I can't bear to be with them."

It was the first verbal acknowledgment that Munsie had ever made of her love for Sam, and Esther patted her helplessly and said, "I understand, Munsie."

But Ish came and helped Hope set the table. He was fifteen, he told himself, and a girl of twelve had no right to make him feel like an awkward fool with her sharp sallies and her quick, barbed laughter. But she did, and he wondered miserably why he was there at all. She was really nothing but a child. But he noted the budding breasts and the growing curves of hips and belly, and wondered if she'd started her period yet, and was ashamed that he thought of it.

During the dinner, Lucy asked Joe when he planned to finish the Mead house. She said it not unkindly, and Joe answered in the same vein, spreading his sensitive doctor's hands. "I don't know, Lucy. That was my black period when I was going to show the world. I think I had some idea of erecting a grand mansion and living it up. Now I couldn't care less." He smiled at Esther.

"He does have some plans though," Esther said. "Tell them, Joe."

"Well, Esther loves this house so. I think we'll remodel it gradually and try to keep the things that are dear to her, like the tall windows and certain pieces of furniture."

"Like the rocker," Esther supplied.

Her husband laughed. "The rocker helps my wife solve her problems. Let something worry her, and off she goes to rock and rock till she's ironed it out in her mind."

"Grandear used to do that," Lucy said wistfully.

"Anyway, later on when we're satisfied here, we want to put up a modest six-unit apartment house on my land. Negroes coming into this city can't find a decent place to rent. Of course, that's still a pipe dream. We don't have the money yet."

"I see you're figuring to be rich," Sam said good-naturedly. "Well, no harm in that, is there, Lucy?"

Lucy shrugged. "Them that has, gets."

Joe lit a pipe and puffed at it speculatively. "You two might think of investing with us by the time we're ready. I mean, suppose it cost us fifty or sixty thousand to build. Even if you could only put in five or six thousand, that'd be ten per cent, and you would share ten per cent of the profits."

"You mean it?" Sam asked, pleased.

"How you know we got five or six thousand?" Lucy asked suspiciously.

Esther said hurriedly, "Well, that's all in the future. Let's drink a toast now to Sam and Lucy and the baby."

They raised their glasses with the domestic champagne. "The little stranger," Hope suggested with mock coyness. "Why, Tattie, you're blushing!"

"You're getting too fresh!" Lucy said hotly.

"And that's a fact!" Ish agreed.

Later that evening, Hope took Lucy to her bedroom to show her a magazine pattern for a dress she hoped to get her to make. And Sam seized the opportunity to ask Joe and Esther about the loan.

Esther said quickly, "But of course, Sam."

But Joe shook his head. "We wouldn't want you in our debt, Sam. Why don't you just let us make you a gift of the three hundred? You've always been so good to Esther and Hope. You can call this our gift to you and Lucy for good luck for the new baby or something. It would make us happy if you'd accept it."

"Please, Sam," Esther urged.

He didn't want to accept it that way, but eventually he agreed. "Lucy may be angry at first. She don't like nobody to go against her. But she'll enjoy going for rides in the evenings. It'll be good for her to get out more, especially now. She won't be mad long," he said hopefully.

Chapter Thirty-three

AS WAS EXPECTED, Lucy did a bit of fussing about the car. She accused them all of conspiring behind her back. The truth was that Lucy hated surprises of any kind; they unnerved her. And Sam hadn't said a word to her until he drove the car up to the door. But once she got used to the idea, it began to give her pleasure to go riding in her own car. The rides in the evenings with her husband gave her a sense of security and helped her not to think about the panic with which she faced her confinement.

At five months, her body was already ungainly, and Lucy asked innumerable questions of Esther. Wasn't she too big for five months? Was it because she was pregnant that she was being bothered with her asthma again? Would they put her to sleep in time so she wouldn't feel the pain?

She rode an uncertain pendulum between high elation over her victory as a woman and depressed irritability at the prospect. At the latter times she was cross and difficult even with Hope, who began to shun her. And her outbursts at Sam were vicious and irrational. Her moods descended on her suddenly.

"God knows I married a knuckle-head. You call yourself a carpenter, and don't know how big your own front door is! Bringing in a tree won't fit in the house!"

"But 'twould have been easy for me to cut it down," Sam said grimly, keeping his hands steady on the wheel.

It was Christmas Eve, a season that Sam loved; but the joy of it was dimmed for him by Lucy's nagging. It was eight o'clock, and he was hungry, for she'd given him no dinner. She was in one of her rages, and nothing would do but for them to drive downtown in the rain to get another tree, while the perfectly good one he'd bought was thrown out in the back yard.

"That old tree was lopsided, anyway," Lucy argued. "I said a little one. You driving so slow, all the trees be gone before we get there. You ain't doing but twenty! You're a spiteful man, Sam Adams! You can go faster than that!"

"The ground is slick, woman!" he shouted at her, his patience gone. "You want to get us killed? Just shut up and let me be! You'll get your tree."

"Don't you talk to me like that, Sam Adams! Don't you say another word!"

They were at an intersection. He turned his head to vent his anger on her, and at that moment a truck loomed out of the side street. Sam turned his wheel sharply to avoid it. The wheels made a sickening screech, skidding wildly towards the curb. There was a thump, and then a soft whirring sound. In a moment, Sam realized that it came from the still revolving wheels of the half-overturned car. He was unhurt, but Lucy was not moving, and there was blood everywhere.

"We couldn't save the child," Dr. Matthews said briskly to Esther. "Pity. But she can still have others."

"And my sister?"

"She's all right. As soon as she gets over her shock. Well, I've got to get back to Main."

"I'm staying with her. If you're needed, you'll come to her, doctor?"

He raised an eyebrow at her. "I'm sure I won't be. But you can call the resident, if necessary."

He was gone. Separate would never be equal, Esther thought. Easy enough to build a new annex, nearly equal in facilities to Main. But how to build an equal measure of concern? An equal measure of respect? The annex was still as far away from Main as ever.

She entered the private room and looked at the drugged and sleeping Lucy, so frail, so hurt, as always so childlike in sleep. Sam sat beside her, exhausted and broken. "It's my fault, Esther," he said to her for the tenth time. "I lost my temper."

She put a hand on his shoulder, but she spoke firmly. "Nonsense! It was an accident, Sam. You'll have more babies. Now go and let the cook give you something to eat. Then lie down in the next room for a while. That's an order! I'm supervisor here, remember?"

He shuffled out as if sleep-walking. Esther moved the heavy hair away from her sister's face and kissed her cheek. "I love you, Lucy," she whispered.

Ellen Dobbins stood in the doorway, beckoning to her. Ellen and her sister Helen wore their roles as nurses' supervisors with dignity, efficiency, and a pleasing humility. They had never forgotten that it was the community, prompted by Ebenezer Baptist Church, that had made it possible for them to be there.

"Why'n't you get some sleep, Miss Kenn—I mean, Mrs. Mead? I'll send Miss Sanders in. She's fairly free. And I'll be in and out."

Esther smiled at her. It was hard to believe that this grave young woman was the giggling, bouncing girl of a few years ago. "I'd rather stay, Ellen. I'd like to be here when she wakes up."

"Well, I'll be here if you need me. I arranged with Miss Head for your shift to be covered. She's sending a white supervisor to relieve me in your place. And after that, Helen comes in, so you don't have to worry."

Esther thanked her. "There is something you can do," she said. "If you'll see after Mr. Adams, my sister's husband. It's been hard on him."

The nurse put her arms about her and hugged her gently. "It's all right, now. We're going to take the best care of your sister, and Mr. Adams too," Ellen whispered. Then, embarrassed, she walked rapidly down the hall in her noiseless white shoes.

Early in the morning, Lucy woke to find her sister sitting beside her. "I lost my baby, didn't I?" she asked, and began to weep pitifully.

"Yes. But you can have others. Don't cry, Lucy. Don't cry, Honey."

Lucy drew away from her touch. "Sam did this to me," she wailed.

"No, darling. You mustn't say that."

"Oh, it's his fault all right. And yours too. Yours too, Esther! You were responsible for him buying that car. You and Joe. Everything I ever wanted you took away from me! Everything!"

"Lucy dear, be reasonable. It wasn't anybody's fault. It was an accident. And there'll be other babies. The doctor said so."

Lucy's face, swollen from crying, assumed a crafty expression. "There won't be any other babies," she said emphatically. "Because, so help me God, Sam Adams won't get to stick his black diddly up in me again. Not till kingdom come!" And she turned her face to the wall, against Esther, and against her husband standing in the doorway with the knife in his heart, because he had heard what she said, and because she had meant him to hear it.

Chapter Thirty-four

"I'm leaving," Esther said to Miss Head, "because I'm pregnant; and even though I'm only three months, my husband insists on it. He's wanted me to stop work for some time." She couldn't help the note of pride in her voice.

Miss Head smiled her brisk smile. "We'll miss you. You've done wonders here. But your husband's right, of course. And now with Ellen and Helen, we can manage. I understand we'll have three other graduate nurses in the annex soon. But I'll be seeing you. You'll have your baby here, won't you?"

"Of course. Miss Head, I want to thank you for—well, for everything. You've been more than kind."

Their eyes held. They had clashed often; but there had grown between them a mutual respect, and what, if the circumstances had been different, might have been friendship.

"I wish you luck, my dear," Miss Head said earnestly, and extended her hand.

Hope was thirteen when Joseph Mitchell Mead was born. He was a big healthy baby with a placid disposition and an engaging smile, much adored by everyone except Hope, who viewed him with indifference, and Lucy, whose sense of justice he outraged. That Esther should become pregnant about the same time that Lucy had lost her own child, seemed to the older sister proof that God was both cruel and blind; and she, ever timid and cautious, now rose up in her heart to shake her fist at Him.

Esther should be hurt as she had been. But how to hurt Esther? She seemed to rise above every circumstance. There was only one way in which Esther could be hurt. Only one way . . .

Lucy never went next door if she could help it, and she discouraged the Meads, with the exception of Hope, from visiting her. Sam, who was now made to sleep on a narrow cot in another room, pitied her and feared for her sanity. Occasionally he forgot to be patient, and shouted at her in his male helplessness. Then she would cry, and he would be remorseful and bewildered.

"If I got to sleep by myself, at least buy me a decent bed to sleep in," he'd plead. Because he took Lucy's increasing stinginess as part of the sickness of her spirit, he'd subside quickly. But he was a simple, lusty man, and his unfulfilled passions made him nervous and depressed.

One night when he came home, Lucy astonished him by saying, "I got myself a job doing part-time cleaning for a white woman." When he exploded, she said calmly, "Only way I can ever have anything is to go out and work for it."

Sam got in his mended car then, and drove the short distance to Munsie's cottage, knowing dimly that she would give understanding. "She never did like nothing much to do with sex," he said haltingly to her. "She just put up with it. But since she lost that baby, she won't let me touch her at all. And now she's trying to make me feel less than a man. I don't know what to do, Munsie. I need a woman."

"I'm a woman, Sam," she said simply.

And seeing the love in her that he had refused to see before, he went, guilty but grateful, into that warm sweet welcoming flesh, finding comfort and, to his amazement, giving it.

Joe was prospering, and he was pleased with his life and the people in it. He had joy in his work, and in his wife, and in the fine son that looked like him. There was only the never-quite-erased shame for the way he had treated his grandfather—the scar on his self-respect that gave him humility. And there was Hope. He had always loved the child, for she was Esther's. But she was difficult and temperamental, and no matter how he tried to show his love for her, she could still by a word or gesture manage to make him feel like an interloper. He had patience with that, but less with the fact that Hope's attitude was a worry to her mother.

Things came to a head on the day he came home to find Esther sitting in the old rocker and crying. Esther didn't cry often, and Joe was alarmed. "Something wrong with Mitch?" He felt a twinge of guilt that that was his first thought. But it wasn't the baby, who was sleeping, thumb in mouth, oblivious to the woes of adults. Esther, cleaning Hope's room, had come across a scrapbook hidden in the back of a closet.

"I'm crying because I'm just plain mad!" she told her husband. "Look at this! She must have cut out every newspaper picture and article they've ever done of Paul and pasted it in here."

Joe examined the book, which was neatly and painstakingly compiled. The front page was inscribed "MY FATHER" with many decorative flourishes and curlicues. "Quite a shrine!" Joe said wryly. "You suppose she sleeps with it under her pillow?"

"Don't joke now, Joe!" Esther spoke sharply. "This is serious. I thought she'd got over this nonsense. How she can revere a man who's never done a thing for her, doesn't know she's alive, and would only be ashamed of her if he did! And she's just barely civil to you, who love her and care for her like your own! Dammit! I ought to beat the devil out of her!"

She was really furious; and because she was, Joe was angry too for her sake. He said, "You'd better let me deal with this, Esther. Where is she now?"

"At Lucy's."

"Well, that's partly the trouble. You let her spend too much time with a woman that's neurotic as hell, and getting worse. Who knows all the tripe Lucy puts in her head? It's got to stop. Hope has to understand we won't put up with this sort of thing."

Hope, coming through the door, said coldly, "Well, what'd I do now?"

"This." Joe held the book up to view.

She flushed, and the hazel eyes darkened. "So you've been snooping!"

"Don't talk to your father like that!" Esther said sternly.

"He's not my father!"

There was a brief silence in which Hope blanched as Joe advanced towards her and stopped. He spoke coldly. "Until you're of age, Hope, and as long as I support you, buy your clothes, and pay for your schooling, I am legally your father. We've had enough of your rudeness. From now on, there will be no reference to any other father in this house." He began methodically, and without anger, to tear the book to pieces, page by page.

Hope's face was drained of color; but she held herself proudly as she answered. "You've no right to do that. He is my real father and I have a right to love him, even if he is white."

Joe looked at her levelly. "You're pretty proud of that, aren't you?"

"Don't, Joe," Esther said. He shouldn't have destroyed the book. Now it was too late to stop them from saying what they would.

"And if I am? It's a white world, isn't it?"

Joe's expression didn't change. His voice was conversational. "My father was white too, Hope. I never knew him at all. In fact, I'm not sure my mother knew exactly who he was. You see, she was what is known as a whore. But I was prouder of her than of him, for she did what she could for me."

Hope was biting her lip, but he went on relentlessly. "You make a point of hurting your mother and me by parading your pride in this white father of yours. Let me tell you, girl, you have no right to be proud. You were born because he raped your mother when she was just three years older than you are now—an innocent girl working in his house. He took her because she was black and he was white, and he could get away with it. The other way around, they'd have strung him up. You have no right to be proud."

Esther was trembling. Joe had said what had to be said. It was not the whole truth; but how to tell the whole truth?

Hope was trembling too. She said, out of her deep and terrible shock, "Mama?" And saw by Esther's face that it was true. She stood for a while, holding herself still. Then she went quietly to her room, and locked the door.

"I must go to her," Esther said. "You were too harsh, Joe."

"No, Esther. You can't shield her forever."

It was what she had said to Grandear. "You can't shield

me forever." He took her hand, and she let him restrain her, for she trusted him.

The next afternoon, Lucy descended on them, a shrieking caricature of an avenging angel. "You have abused that child! And I want you to know it's somebody here who'll take up for her!"

"She had to be told," Esther said warily.

"Ha! Told things to make her feel like she was nothing? 'Tweren't no harm in her having feelings for her father."

Joe spoke. "Yes, there was, Lucy. Those feelings were destroying her. She was thinking her white blood was making her something special among Negroes. Hope has to find herself as a person, not as black or white or mulatto."

She turned on him. "*You're* destroying her! You hate her because Esther had her by another man—a rich white man at that! But I'll tell you something. You can't keep that child from knowing her heritage. Like Grandear said, 'Deep calleth unto deep'; and the white blood in that child's veins will call to her and call to her, just like something in Esther called to something in that boy she say raped her. And it *will call,* and *will call,* until it is answered. And ain't nothing you can do to stop it!"

Lucy backed out of the door, pointing like the wrath of God. With her final word, the door slammed shut behind her. Esther and Joe looked at each other in sheer amazement.

Hope had as little as possible to do with Mitch. It was her way of punishing her parents for wounding her. Esther felt that she needed time, and didn't force her to help with the baby. But occasionally, curiosity got the better of the girl. One day, Esther was bathing the child, and Hope came into the room and sat silently nearby watching the proceedings. Esther dried her happily cooing son and turned to her. "How about dressing him for me?"

"Do I have to?"

"No. But you'll have your own one day. It won't hurt to practice a little on your brother."

Hope hesitated the right length of time to show her lack of eagerness before she complied. When she did, she handled the infant with dexterity. Esther smiled and left the room briefly. When she returned, Mitch, powdered and diapered, was being gently rocked and crooned to by his sister. "He's the sweetest, goodest baby, ain't him?" Hope halted, embarrassed and annoyed at being caught so.

"You were pretty special too, you know," Esther said.

"I bet I wasn't spoiled like this one." There was a wistful note in the girl's voice.

"Oh, much more! You were so outrageously pretty, in the first place. And then you were my first-born."

Hope's eyes met her mother's, searchingly. Esther went to sit beside her on the bed. She spoke conversationally. "You'll find out when you have your own, Hope. A mother loves all her children, naturally. But she has a special place for her first child. No matter how many others she has, she remembers the wonder of that first baby."

Hope said nothing.

"I love you very much, Hope," Esther said, feeling desperate. "And your—Joe loves you too."

"I know," Hope said surprisingly. Her face convulsed then, and she handed the child back to his mother. "It's not you at all, Mama! It's me!" she cried. And she ran from the room, bursting into passionate tears.

Mitch, so abruptly deposited, began to wail too. Esther soothed him. At thirteen, Grandear had said, girls were all glands and foolish notions. But it would be all right. Hope had found and faced the enemy within. But hers would be a long fight. Esther prayed to know how to help her.

Chapter Thirty-five

THERE CAME a Saturday, the first in April, when suddenly, as happens in the South, it was spring. The day itself, warm and jewel-bright, held for Hope an underlying excitement. She felt that something different and wonderful should happen on a day like that. It was not a day to go shopping for groceries with her mother. If she did, she'd be saddled with Mitch, who loved to pull at things on shelves. It was not a day to read, nor to visit with the girls she knew. She didn't feel like snickering and giggling about nothing, the way they did. It was a day to ponder life and its mysteries, to make some vital discovery.

But, after much consideration, she could find nothing better to do than to take a solitary walk. She thought of going to the hill. But that was not new nor far; and now that she was nearly fourteen, it had lost much of its enchantment for her. As she walked down the streets of the familiar neighborhood, her discontent grew. There was little of loveliness there. Most of the old wooden houses needed painting; the porches sagged; and the housewives who waved to her from them looked as bedraggled as the chickens who pecked in their untidy gardens.

Why didn't the colored sections of town look like the white? Why were colored people trapped in such squalor? Where she was going resolved itself then. It would take her about an hour to walk to the house where her Aunt Lucy worked. Tattie would be through about that time, and they could ride back on the bus together. Along the way, she would look at the houses and lawns that looked the way houses and lawns should look. She would pretend as she walked that she lived in a neighborhood like that.

David Chase, only child of his parents, both dreamer and rebel, was also made restless by the excitement of the day. It was a day to ponder life and its mysteries, to make some vital discovery. To David, life and its mysteries meant LOVE in capital letters. It irked him that at sixteen he still had no great yearning for any girl, no terrible, all-consuming passion that would transform him from boy to man, from dreamer to knower. Not that he couldn't toss off as many stories of his experiences as the rest of the fellows. But that was a different thing. He showed his lesser self to the world, as expected; but the private, splendidly sensitive self was his glory, to be shared only with that one, beautiful of soul as he, whom he would know on sight. He took an apple, a pen, and a notebook, small enough to be pocketed quickly, and went out onto the front lawn, sat under a tree, and began to write a poem.

He hadn't seen the girl come through the gate. He didn't see her at all until she spoke to him. "Excuse me. Is Lucy Adams here?" And her voice was a soft tinkle. He looked up dazedly, because he had just written, "Her soft voice sunders my heart."

She was not real. No flesh and blood girl could be that exquisite! He sat up on an elbow and stared at her. His eyes traveled the length of her, seeing in a glance the shiny brown hair, caught into a neat pony-tail, the supple golden body in the pink cotton dress, the bare legs glistening with tiny golden hairs, the perfect pink-tipped toes in the flat pink sandals. But it was her face that he found incredible. It was the heart-shaped face that in his dream he had ascribed to the one whom his soul would know—more beautiful in reality than in his imaginings.

But as he gazed into the great light-flecked hazel eyes, he came to himself with a sickening onrush of reality. This girl was not the one. She was, beautiful or not, a Negro.

If he had said the thing that came to his mind then, he

would have been spared what came later. It would have been easy enough to say, "Yes, Lucy's here. If you want to see her, go around the back way." But he said instead, "You ring the bell and she'll answer. Nobody else is in. Are you related to her or something?"

"I'm her niece," Hope said, and smiled at him before she went, for he had the blackest hair, the whitest skin, and the bluest eyes she had ever seen. He was handsome, and he had looked at her from his sensitive face in the way that meant he found her lovely. She walked with conscious grace to the front door, feeling his eyes on her as she went.

"What you doing here?" Lucy asked.

"I thought you'd like company going back."

Lucy was pleased, but nervous. It had been a shock to open the white folks' front door and find Hope standing there. "How come you didn't come to the back?"

"Well, the boy said I should ring the bell."

"Mister David?"

"Is that his name?" Lucy marked the touch of excitement in the girl's voice.

As they were leaving, David was standing nonchalantly at the back gate. "You'll be back Monday, Lucy?"

He had never before said two words to her. She answered in surprise. "No, I only come Tuesdays, Thursdays, and Saturdays, Mr. David." But he and Hope were looking at each other. And suddenly Lucy understood. She said, "Come on, Hope. That bus only runs every half-hour."

On the bus, Lucy was silent for a long time, as was Hope. Each was thinking her own secret thoughts—Hope's a little sad, Lucy's a little mad.

When Lucy spoke finally, she said brightly, "Sugar, it's nice to have company home. This can be a lonesome ride. Maybe you ought to come pick me up oftener. Next time though, come the back way."

Still at the gate, David was thinking, "Hope. It fits. If we lived somewhere else . . . Segregation surely the mark of a decadent society . . . Only the young and the visionary . . . How old was she? Fourteen? Fifteen at the most . . . but beautiful . . . beautiful . . . Come again, Hope . . . Come soon . . ."

Esther, in the supermarket, was also feeling the excitement of the day; and she laughed with Mitch, sharing his glee in the multitude of tins and boxes and faces, not knowing that Lucy, the mad prophet, having made her prediction, was finding a way to make it come true.

Chapter Thirty-six

JOE STRENUOUSLY objected to Hope's Saturday afternoon walks to the Chase house. He and Esther had their first major quarrel about it.

It happened on a Saturday in June when Esther was out of sorts. Mitch, besides cutting two new teeth, had caught a cold and was demanding and irritable. The washing machine had broken down and Esther had to do the clothes by hand. Then she forgot the roast in the oven and eventually found it burned to a crisp.

Esther never admitted it, but she chafed under the routine of housework. She missed her job—the sense of purpose and usefulness it gave her. As much as she loved her family, she was not geared to being exclusively a housewife, and at times like these the strain told in her relationship with Joe.

He came home from the office that afternoon, tired because Saturday was always his busiest day—the day on which people from neighboring villages and farms came to town, did their shopping, and visited the doctor if necessary.

"Anything to eat?" he asked.

"No, and won't be for a while," she answered flatly.

"Well, good Lord, Esther! You knew I'd be home at five. I've worked like hell today, and I'm starving!"

She bristled. "So make yourself a sandwich, if you can't wait. For your information, I've worked like hell, too. Besides everything else going wrong, Mitch is driving me wild. I only five minutes ago got him to take a nap."

He sat on the kitchen stool and regarded her with some amusement. She was chopping onions furiously, and the tears came as much from them as from frustration. "Steady, girl! I'll wait for dinner. Suppose you stop a while and have a beer with me. We both need it."

He took the cans from the refrigerator, opened them expertly, and handed her one. "Now sit down and tell Papa your troubles."

It was something she loved about him, the way he could soothe her out of a black mood. She laughed ruefully. "I just had a rough day, that's all. I should have stayed in bed." She explained what had happened.

He eyed her thoughtfully. "Esther, why don't you make Hope help you more? She's old enough to carry her weight around here."

Her waning resentment flared anew. There were times when she felt that Joe interfered too much in her handling of Hope. "Joe, I can't be too strict with her. She's had a bad enough time as it is. She's not even fourteen yet. She does well in school, and if her worst fault at her age is laziness around the house, we've a lot to be thankful for."

Her irritation was contagious. "Where is she now?" he asked stiffly.

"She went to meet Lucy."

He frowned. "You mean at the place where Lucy works?"

"Yes."

"Esther, I've been meaning to say this to you. I don't like the idea of Hope walking around by herself in a white neighborhood."

"She's not walking around. She goes straight there and rides back with Lucy. What could happen to her?"

Joe set his beer down to shake his head wonderingly at her. "Esther, you amaze me! Sometimes I swear I'm married to a white chick from Alaska!"

She pulled her lip to a point. "What d'you mean by that?"

He ignored the danger signal. "You've lived all your life a black woman in the South; and for all you've been through, you haven't let it touch you at all. You don't seem to know what it's all about! It hasn't even occurred to you that a pretty Negro girl like Hope could come to harm alone in a white area?"

"Not in broad daylight, Joe," she said impatiently. "And I don't want Hope to grow up in fear. That's the trouble with us down here. We've all been too afraid too long. Too much fear, and too much hate. I won't teach my child that."

He narrowed his eyes, and said quietly, "You'd better teach *my* child that, Esther. You have some fine and fancy theories about there being good in all men. Maybe as a woman, you need to feel like that to survive emotionally. But the Negro man in the South can't afford any such nice illusions. He must see the white man for what he is—one who exploits, and rapes, and murders! One who teaches fear!"

His voice rose. "Most of us have learned our lessons well, Esther. We've learned so much fear that we've finally learned to hate. I mean hate from our guts! And it's a beautiful thing, that hate. I'll tell you, girl, there's enough hate in the guts of black men all over the world to blow every white bastard to hell. It's been a long time coming, but there are signs everywhere, and I glory to see the day! By the time that child in there is grown, he'll glory in his blackness. Esther, hate born of fear is my son's heritage, and his hope

[143]

of glory. And don't you dare try to fill his head with this nonsense about brotherhood and the white man's basic goodness!"

She had never before come so full face with this violence in her husband. She had seen only the sheathed blade. Now it frightened her. She stood up. "He's my son too," she said. "Although it's convenient for you to disown Hope whenever it suits you, they're both my children. I've seen what this hate you glory in has done to you and a lot of others. It's put something twisted and ugly in you. You may say that it's only for the white man; but it carries over into everything you say and do and think. I won't let that happen to my children, or to me. Joe, how can you, a doctor who's supposed to heal, be so full of destruction?"

He laughed shortly. "Sugar, every time I bring a black child into the world, every time I heal a sick black body, I think this is one more member for the black army."

She said earnestly, "This hate will destroy you before it can reach out to destroy the white man."

"There you go again with your theories! Hell, you have been brain-washed, haven't you? Can't you see how the white man has capitalized on his hatreds? He's grown rich and powerful on his prejudices. Hate niggers enough, and you can kill any conscience about exploiting them. When our turn comes, we damn well better not have any conscience either."

Esther stared at him. "It's still evil and terrible, whoever does the hating. And, so help me God, Joe, on this one thing I'll fight you till I die! I won't let it happen to Hope or Mitch!"

He said tiredly, "It doesn't happen, Esther. It's deliberately injected into the blood, day by day, year by year. A slow poison of humiliation and terror. Anything that happens is only a symptom. You can't be black and immune to it. You can't protect Hope or Mitch from it. The white man's needleful of hate is longer than your mother love, Esther. Some day you'll find even yourself full of it. Poor darling! What'll you do then?"

She was tired of being torn in two directions. What she said then in a calm sensible tone was all the more hurtful because of its seed of truth. "Joe, are you certain all this fuss isn't because you simply resent Hope's attachment to Lucy? To anyone, for that matter. Even to me."

He widened his eyes. "Girl, you have lost your mind!"

"Well, you must admit that you're jealous because you haven't been able to win her to you. So you go on about *your* son and *my* daughter. And whenever something comes up about Hope, you raise the roof. But don't you think it's a little foolish to be jealous of Lucy? After all, Hope owes a lot to her aunt. Lucy was there helping me with her long before you ever decided to come around." She stopped, stricken. The thing that had driven her vanished, and she saw clearly what she had said. "I'm sorry. I shouldn't have said that!" she cried.

But it was too late. He got up and left the room, the house. He didn't come home until after midnight. When he did, he was very drunk. Sunday morning, they made it up in a desperate abandon of love-making. But it was a surface healing, and they both knew it.

Esther cried on Munsie's shoulder on Monday morning, when her old friend voluntarily came to help.

"A wife promises to obey her husband," Munsie reminded her sternly. "Besides, he's right on most counts, Esther. Hope is too young and too pretty to be going out there. And Lucy is too hard to figure to be let alone with that child, good as she's been to her."

They would tread carefully around the subject of Lucy. Esther, with her acute female instinct, guessed that Munsie and Sam were having an affair. She appreciated the delicacy on Munsie's part that made her visits now a rarity. She had come today only because she had heard that Mitch was sick. That morning, she'd done the washing. Esther, despite her loyalty to Lucy, could not condemn this staunch and beloved friend for what she merely guessed at.

"I guess you're right," Esther said. "Lucy is in a bad way. But Hope seems to help her."

"What I'm worried about is that she'll harm Hope," Munsie said heavily.

"If Joe had agreed to let Hope alone, she'd probably stop going soon enough. I suppose I'll have to forbid her; but now she'll probably feel it's just another thing we're doing to make her miserable. And Lucy will probably think we're doing it to spite her."

They hadn't heard Lucy come in. Esther never locked doors when the weather was good, and Lucy had taken to walking in noiselessly, often catching her unawares. Esther was startled now to see her standing in the kitchen doorway.

"How long've you been standing there, Lucy?"

Lucy's lip curled. She said shrilly and with much satisfaction, "Long enough to hear you discussing me with this whore."

Munsie's manner was menacing. "If I wasn't in your sister's house, I'd make you take back that word, Lucy. But I got too much respect for Esther."

Lucy didn't look at her. She addressed herself exclusively to Esther. "You need to have some respect for yourself. Gossiping about me with my husband's whore."

Esther's heart began a wild hammering.

"I know she thinks I don't know about it," Lucy went on loudly. "But I got eyes and ears. She been wanting him for many a year. But one thing is sure; she didn't get him till I turned him out my bed. And if I let him back in at any time, she wouldn't have him no more."

Munsie stood up, breathing heavily. She said bitterly, "I didn't mean no harm to you, Lucy. And I didn't never ask Sam to come to me. But since he did, I ain't never going to ask him to leave! He can come to my bed whenever he wants. He's a good man, Sam is. He respects me and my boy. Won't come at all when Ish is home. And I acts like a woman to him, which is more than you ever done. And since you know so much, you may as well know that I love him, and he loves me too. And ain't nothing you can do about that!"

She was crying noiselessly as she spoke; but she left with her head proud and high. "Bitch!" Lucy yelled after her. But Munsie didn't turn.

"Lucy, Lucy!" Esther said sadly. "Why must you always hurt and tear down?"

Her sister stared at her oddly. "Because *I'm* hurt and torn down," Lucy said.

Chapter Thirty-seven

HOPE CARRIED her secret in triumph and in fear. The white boy was in love with her. She knew it. He had said that she was beautiful and that he dreamed of her at night. Once in their whispered conversations, he had called her "my other self. My lovely other self!" And she loved him too. Even thinking of him set her tingling and glowing so that she had to hide the way she was feeling from her parents' discerning eyes.

In some corner of her mind she wondered at Lucy's obvious blindness to what was happening. She and David never spoke to each other if his parents were home, but they seldom were on Saturday afternoons; and while Hope waited for Lucy she would wander into the hallway and

David would meet her there, casually. And they would talk, softly. At first, Hope had lived in fear of Lucy's discovery. But after several such meetings, that her aunt surely knew about but never interrupted, Hope forgot to be nervous. It seemed at such times that Lucy took longer than ever to get ready. It was impossible that this was deliberate. Still, it was strange. Maybe fate or God was helping them. So she'd thought until that morning when Esther had forbidden her to go again. Esther had made no mention of Joe, but Hope knew he had a hand in it, and she hated him.

Hope and David stood in the hall, swaying towards each other, quivering and awkward in their young tenderness, and held back because Lucy was in the next room.

Hope said, restraining her tears, "I won't see you again. My mother says I can't come here any more. She only let me come today because I'd promised Aunt Lucy."

He blanched. "You must come! I mean—well, isn't there somewhere else we can meet?"

After a moment, she asked, "If I knew a place, would you think badly of me?"

"Don't you know I worship you?" he asked softly.

"You wouldn't take advantage of me?"

"How could I, Hope?"

She lowered her eyes. "They say white boys only want one thing from a colored girl. I'd hate you if you were like that!"

"I'm not like that, Hope. You think your being colored means anything to me? Oh, God! I'd reverence you as much as a white girl. More! I love you, Hope. How I love you!"

She lifted her eyes to his. "I know a place," she said slowly. "You could meet me there tomorrow."

In the next room, Lucy listened with a dawning horror at what was happening, and a fearful fascination at the thing inside herself that would not let her stop it.

Chapter Thirty-eight

As USUAL, the Meads and the Adamses went to church together on Sunday morning. Munsie and Ish always sat in the pew immediately behind. Today, Munsie hesitated before deciding not to make a change. For Ishmael's sake she had to act normally, as long as Lucy would let her. She was relieved, when the service was over, that Lucy said nothing to her or about her. Lucy had other things on her mind.

As was their habit in public, Sam and Munsie said only a polite hello, and immediately Munsie shifted her eyes to her son. She was never quite sure that Ishmael didn't know what was going on. But if he did, he gave no sign of it. Ishmael was mature beyond his years, having learned early to accept things as they were. He was talking now with Hope on the church steps. "You want me to come over this afternoon?"

"No. Not today, Ish." No one but Lucy detected the panic in her voice.

"Don't be rude, Hope," Esther said. "Of course you may come, Ish. Stay to dinner."

He looked at his mother, who said quickly, "You go on. I can't come, Esther. I got to break the Sabbath. I ain't caught up on the white folks' washing, and it's due tomorrow."

Lucy's lip curled, but she said nothing. She was watching Hope in her concealed desperation. Only Sam, silent and sad, saw the gleam in his wife's eyes, and wondered what lay behind it.

Joe, holding his restless son, genially invited Sam and Lucy to come to dinner too, and only after Lucy's quick acceptance saw Esther biting her lip, which meant she was annoyed. Esther had been feeling particularly happy, for she and Joe were in harmony that morning and very tender towards each other. She did not want Sam and Lucy to dinner. But she knew Joe had invited them to show how he felt, and she could only second the invitation.

When they sat down to dinner, Hope wasn't there. When the meal was over, she was still not to be found.

"I can't imagine where she disappeared to," Esther said in annoyance. "She was helping me in the kitchen. Then I sent her to wash up and I haven't seen her since."

"Maybe she slipped out to visit one of her friends," Ishmael ventured.

"Just before dinner, and not saying a word to me? Did she say anything to you, Joe?"

Her husband shook his head. "Don't upset yourself, Esther. She must be somewhere in the neighborhood."

"But it isn't like her to go off like that!"

"I shouldn't have come," Ishmael said sadly. "She said she didn't want me."

"I'm sorry, Ish," Esther said. "It's not your fault. She's too old for whippings now, but we'll have to punish her for this. It's rude of her."

"Maybe she just wanted to be alone for a while," Sam said, trying to be helpful. "Sometimes girls her age are like that."

Lucy giggled, and everyone looked at her. She was sitting slackly in her chair, but her hands were clenched into fists on the table. The giggle grew in volume till her body shook uncontrollably with the sounds that came from her open mouth. But her face held no mirth, and her eyes were wild.

Sam got up and shook her roughly by the shoulders. "Stop it, Lucy! Stop it!"

"Joe, she's sick! Do something!" Esther cried.

Joe, the doctor, immediately calm and efficient, went to her. "Come now, Lucy," he said, taking her hand. "Come and lie down for a while, and we'll see what's the matter."

She shook him off and the giggling stopped abruptly, giving way to a weird calm. She rose and pointed a finger at Esther. "You wouldn't listen to me. But I told you! I warned you her white blood would call to her, and when it called she would answer! Today she has answered, Esther, my fine sister. Today she has answered!" Her voice was sepulchral.

Esther sat rooted to the seat. She said in a whisper, "How has she answered, Lucy?"

Lucy nodded sagely. "They thought I didn't hear them, whispering in the halls, holding hands in the kitchen." She laughed shortly, and her voice grew petulant as a child's. "I'm no fool! Everybody tries to play me for a fool. But I saw them whispering. I heard them! Ha! I didn't say a word. She went to meet him. Black Hope Kennedy and white David Chase! Ha, ha! How you like that, Esther? How you like that, my fine sister?"

Sam said, "Oh, God! Where's she meeting him, Lucy? Tell me, woman!"

But Lucy smiled at him, closed her lips, and sat down.

Joe and Esther looked at each other. They spoke simultaneously. "The hill!"

Ishmael sat alone at the dining-room table, holding the wailing Mitch on his knees. "You mustn't cry now, Mitch. They'll be back soon. And your sister's all right. Don't worry. She's all right." And he was glad that the child was too young to care that he was bawling too.

"I love you for coming to me," David said. "Did you have any trouble getting out?"

"Not much." She wished she weren't so nervous. "Did you have trouble getting here?"

"Well, the bus driver asked what I was doing in South Leemouth."

"What'd you tell him?"

"That I was on an errand for my father."

What he'd actually said was that he'd been sent to give the cook her wages, because she was sick. But he couldn't tell Hope that. She was acutely sensitive on the subject of color. "It's nice here. Very secluded—and beautiful," he added hastily. "You come here often?"

"I used to."

"Oh?" He fell silent, and she turned anxious, puzzled eyes on him, pulling her dress a little further down to cover her knees. "I never before brought anybody up here," she said pointedly.

He flushed. "Don't you think I know that?"

"I don't know. Maybe I shouldn't have let you come." Her voice faltered. "I don't guess it looks right."

He searched her fresh, troubled face, and his vague misgivings yielded abruptly to an overwhelming tenderness. "Don't be sorry, Hope," he said earnestly. "I'd never hurt you or shame you in any way. You know that!"

She nodded, seeing the truth of it in his eyes; but she was still uneasy, and an awkward silence lengthened between them.

"It's a nice day," he said desperately at last.

"Yes."

They looked at each other, and simultaneously began to giggle. What they had said was all suddenly absurd in the bright sunlight with their youth, and their innocence, and their love shimmering about them. Still giggling, they threw themselves down on the tall grass. And they kissed, still trembling a bit on the edge of their laughter, until laughter left because of the quiet radiance of that kiss.

And Esther found them so.

Much later she remembered the purity of the faces they turned to her. She didn't see it at the time, nor care to. Silent and intent, she was upon the boy, her fingers strong, obedient to her single, total hatred, squeezing at the white throat, squeezing the life from every soft, white, boy throat.

"Esther! Stop it! You'll kill him!" Joe wrenched her away. The boy stared dazedly, pitifully, at them for a moment.

"It isn't like you think," he said in a hoarse whisper. Then as Esther made a violent move, he fled, darting like a crouched hare between them, holding his throat, and not once looking back.

Suddenly, Esther had no thought for the boy. It was her child, staring at her with wide, unbelieving eyes, staring with horror at her mother's hands still shaped for murder.

"Oh, God! You're horrible!" Hope whispered.

Esther's fingers went limp as she put out her arms. "Baby! Baby!" she pleaded.

But Hope, who was half kneeling, rose uncertainly and backed away. "You have a dirty mind, Mother. I think I'll always hate you for this." Her voice was flat, toneless.

Then Lucy laughed, the guttural sound of the deranged. Hope turned terrified eyes on her—on them all: on Lucy, trembling in her idiotic laughter; on Sam, making ineffectual shushing noises to restrain her; on Joe and Esther, for the moment frozen in their helplessness. Then she spun on her heels and fled running, running in her little pink sandals down the steep side of the hill, heedless of the brambles and bushes that drew blood from her face and arms—running blindly away from the faces and voices that were now alien—running and not knowing that her legs carried her straight to the railroad tracks.

Lucy, with her mad ears, heard the whistle of the train before it sounded, and was suddenly and hideously sane. "No, Hope!" she cried. "No, Baby!" And terror lent wings to her feet, outdistancing the others easily. She cried as she ran, "Stop, Baby! Stop, darling! Oh, stop, precious Baby!"

Love—the relentless, the terrible, the unmerciful, the at-last-victorious—multiplied her strength, and she caught the beloved in her arms, threw her clear as the black iron fury descended. It didn't matter at all then to Lucy that her heel was caught in the track.

The engineer thought at first he had braked in time. The woman had got the girl out of the way. Then, it seemed, she'd just stood there, taking the final lurch of the engine. If he could have stopped just five seconds sooner! What the hell! How many nigger women were trying to get themselves killed that day?

Esther, holding her unconscious child in her arms, was not aware of the voices and people around her. She was listening to an eerie, keening wail. She had heard it before, long ago. Where? It was Grandear's voice, that sound coming from her own mouth, wailing in terror and despair, "Oh, Gawd! Oh, Gawd! Oh, Gawd!"

And somewhere, a muffled echo of her own chant—Sam, holding his wife's mangled body and sobbing, "Oh, Gawd, Lucy! Oh, Gawd, Lucy!"

Chapter Thirty-nine

THE CRUEL summer passed, the gaudy autumn. Somehow the winter was kinder. It was fitting that earth have its period of mourning with the human heart. Esther bore each successive day as it came to cover the wounds of the past with the patient alchemy of slow forgetting. The lost were inevitably recovered, she learned.

Lucy, lost to the wide silence, buried in the lot that also held her mother and grandmother, was to be found now in small and pleasant things—curtains that she had made in a happier time, a recipe written in her own hand—to be found too in the very existence of Hope, for love of whom she was both saved and destroyed.

Lucy would sleep peacefully, for if she had lived poorly, she had died well.

Sam, lost for a time to his grief and his vague guilts, would be found at last by Munsie, who had had the wisdom merely to wait. They would be married, as Munsie said, "soon as his mind knows what his heart does—that however it is, life's for making the best we can of it."

Hope's losses were too great to be soon recovered, Esther knew. To lose David was to lose what she never could have had. But it was too soon yet for Hope to understand that. Her aunt had died to save her, and in that instant Hope had lost forever the mark of the child—the freedom from personal responsibility for all human tragedy.

Hope would not heal through Esther's efforts, nor Joe's. The girl had been shown too clearly the common frailty of all mortals. In one terrifying afternoon she had learned how little light and salvation were to be found in others. Through the long months as she walked her agonized interior path, she walked alone. Esther, remembering how it had been during her own inward travail after Grandear had died, could only wait and pray. Ishmael, Munsie's child, intelligent and compassionate, waited also. It was Ishmael who already was gaining Hope's first new trust. Perhaps that was only good and right, Esther thought humbly. Through him, eventually Hope might be restored to her.

For herself, there was Joe. That she, who loved well, could hate as fully; that her hands which could heal could also kill—these were all of a piece to Joe, because of whose constant love she learned slowly to accept herself.

Over them all was a bleak peace. It was a time of waiting.

They sat together so on a Sunday afternoon in February over a game of Chinese checkers—Joe, Esther, Hope, Ishmael, Munsie, Sam—playing with neither disinterest nor enthusiasm. It was something to do.

In the next room, two-year-old Mitch slept, oblivious to the cares of adults.

When the phone rang, Joe rose lazily to answer it.

"I hope that's not a patient," Esther said, sighing. Joe seldom had an uninterrupted evening at home.

"If that's Mrs. Armstrong, calling for you to go see 'bout her blessed child again, just tell her the best remedy is to hold his head under water 'bout five minutes," Munsie said, chuckling as she passed over six marbles in one move.

"Oh, shoot! I opened that one up for you," Hope said, biting her lip. "Your move, Ish."

"Hey, Ish! That blue marble's mine," Sam said.

No one was listening to Joe's end of the telephone conversation. But Esther was instantly alert as she heard him say, "Yes, Miss Head. I'll be there immediately. Yes, I know Esther'll come too."

"What is it, Joe?" Esther asked quietly as he hung up.

"The annex. Nearly forty cases of ptomaine. Some banquet or other. They're flooded over there! Esther, you'll be needed. Miss Head said she asks you as a special favor."

But Esther was already on her feet. "I'll get my things."

Munsie chuckled as Esther left for the bedroom. "Lookit that one go! Once a nurse! Joe, you-all be needing my help? I'm pretty good in emergencies. I follow directions good. I'll be glad to come."

"Yes," Joe said. "You too, Ishmael. You too'll be worth ten frantic nurses' aids."

Sam said honestly, "I'd come, but I ain't much good around sick folks with my clumsy self. Maybe I just better stay around here and help Hope with Mitch."

Esther, returning to the room wearing her coat, smiled at him. "Thanks a lot, Sam."

"I want to come too," Hope said.

Everyone turned to look at her, surprised.

"You're sure, Hope?" Esther asked. "It's not going to be pretty."

"I know that."

"In fact, it'll be pretty revolting."

Hope countered with a question. "Then why're you going? You don't have to, either."

Their eyes held.

"Yes I do, dear," Esther answered simply. "I'm a nurse, and people need me. I *have* to help."

"And I *want* to help, Mama," Hope said quietly.

Was it that in truth, or mere curiosity? Hope had too long obscured herself from them all for Esther to be sure. However it was, the girl seemed determined, and Esther was pleased.

"I'll get your coat," Ishmael said.

Munsie nodded gravely. "I'm glad you want to come, Hope. We're all needed. We cain't none of us make it in this world alone, sick or well, rich or poor, black or white."

It was something she had heard before, a long time past, Esther remembered. Mr. Trimble? Or had Grandear said it?

They were silent as Joe drove them quickly and carefully to the hospital. During the next hours there would be little time for other thought than what was at hand to do.

It was warm in the car. Esther let her window down a trifle. A little rush of air flung itself at her face. She shivered with a sudden small delight. It was only February. But already it smelled of spring.